What people are saying:

"*A Suitcase Full of Dried Fish and other stories* is a collection of twelve poignant stories about life in Africa and beyond. They would grab you and will not let you go until you read all of them. Skilfully crafted by Edmonton-based Sierra Leonean-Canadian writer Bakar Mansaray, the fast-moving stories glow with humour and hum with pathos as they take you to the bosom of Mother Africa and the African Diaspora, pulsating with both honey and hemlock, tears and laughter. They are in essence a sharp and unrelenting artistic portrayal of the human condition."

Gibril Gbanabome Koroma,
Editor/Publisher, the Patriotic Vanguard newspaper

"This book of short stories brings back vivid memories of my life as a young boy growing up in Cameroon. It is well written."

Frankline Agbor,
Producer, Diversity Magazine

"We have known the author for few years and Bakar Mansaray's story telling skills left no doubt in my mind that he could put this book together. The title of the book, *A Suitcase Full of Dried Fish and other stories*, is a very fascinating one. It reminds us as Sierra Leoneans in the Diaspora of our main source of protein while growing up in Africa. It is a title that captivates one's interest to read the whole book. All twelve stories speak volumes of who we are as a people and what we endured and had fun with prior to our relocation in the Diaspora. Reading the stories reconnects us to our roots. Get a copy, you won't regret it!"

Monty Domingo
Chairman,
The Sierra Leone Community Association, Ottawa, Canada

A Suitcase full of Dried Fish

and other stories

A Suitcase full of Dried Fish

and other stories

BAKAR MANSARAY

Mandingo Scrolls Series

A Suitcase Full of Dried Fish
And Other Stories

Copyright © Bakar Mansaray, 2015
Illustrations © Aruna Deen Stro, 2015

First published: 2015
Revised Edition 2016

ISBN 978-9-99-105428-5

Cataloguing data available from the Sierra Leone Library Board, Freetown

This is a work of fiction. All of the characters, organizations, and events portrayed in these stories are either products of the author's imagination or are used fictitiously.

Sierra Leonean Writers Series

For Lhamin, Akiatu, Mariama and Ibrahim

Je pensais que l'on devait pourvoir créer une littérature qui refléte simplement notre manière d'être, qui soit un miroir de notre âme et de notre culture.

I was thinking that one should be able to create literature that simply reflects our way of life; that will be a mirror of our soul and our culture.

— *Aminata Sow Fall,*
2015 Grand prize recipient,
Francophonie of the French Academy

Contents

Foreword

The publication of this book, *A Suitcase Full of Dried Fish and other stories*, opens yet another window for a glance into the lives of people. The book presents a vivid account of sociological intricacies. It is an excellent piece of narrative portraying culture, adventure, romance, and amusement. The stories range from the riddles of online dating to the qualms of ill health, and a foretaste of resurrection. The author focuses on resilience as the cornerstone of success, even amidst hardship.

I found this book interesting. It reminds me of the rich cultural experience I had in my native home, Sierra Leone, and during my travels around the African continent. The book is a great tranquilizer for easing nostalgia and so will make a great read for people in the Diaspora in particular and also for amusement-seeking readers in general.

Dr. Abu Conteh
Environmental Biologist
Department of Biological Sciences
MacEwan University
Edmonton, Alberta, Canada

Editor's Preface

This is a collection of incredibly diverse stories—from the very humane story of the grim life of a prostitute who finally contracts the dreaded Human Immunodeficiency Virus; to the troubling tale of the predator-prey food chain of the online eco-system; to the harrowing accounts of war; to the political intrigues of the sit-tight, despotic ruler of a satirical Republic 'where politics was not for the pure in heart'; to the vagaries and hardships of illegal immigration; and even a little bit of chilly supernatural narration that follows a protagonist beyond the grave into the afterlife. Think whodunits, think polygamy, think romance, think about life and living and you will find the author has included a story in this book that will satisfy your taste.

This book gives you the impression of an author who has lived life rather robustly; a keen observer looking at the world with surprisingly attentive eyes. It supplies you insightful glimpses into relationships and allows you to see life with eyes washed in salve. It proves beyond doubt that 'life as a challenge to be conquered' and yet is truly soothing in the way the author tackles each challenge his characters face with a sympathetic pen.

The stories almost always resolve in a way that will leave readers the much-needed assurance that there is an overriding sense of justice in this troubling world of ours: the internet's painful bytes recede when a deserting husband comes home (*Online Dating Comes to Accra*); just two miles from the prostitute's enclave there is a welcoming arm for a prodigal daughter and new life springs from a seemingly dead situation (*Virginia's Triple Cocktail*); from a bitter polygamous home a woman finds salvation in selfless love (*Polygamy*); perpetuators of evil face the long arm of justice (*Murder in Koidu Town & The Monrovia Woman*), a migrant defeats and purges himself of the evil of racial hate (*A Jamaican in Canada*); in the title story (*A Suitcase Full of Dried Fish*), Foday makes it despite that things threaten to spoil along the way; and, even when death sometimes ends a good cause, it becomes obvious that it is not so selectively after all in ending evil causes as well (*Republic of Ugosoba*).

Bakar Mansaray's dexterous storytelling is at once trenchant and light, the stories imaginative and ordinary, the anecdotes singular and well-worn—paradoxes which brought many refreshingly surprising moments to me and made working on this book very satisfying. I trust this book will bring many pleasant reading moments to you too.

Efioanwan Fifi Edem
July 2015

Author's Preface

The genesis of this book of short stories stems from baffling questions for which I seek answers. Have I found the answers to these questions by writing this book? Well, you have to find out as a reader who enjoys entertaining stories.

Some of these questions revolve around the ramifications of Mankind's insatiable desire for love, money and power. Others delve into the polygamous nature of human beings, the enshrined injustices of a world seemingly succumbing to greed, war and disease. If you have ever wondered why so many of us dislike the rigours of existence yet shiver at the mention of the word death, then read this book.

Due to the short nature of these stories, they will be beneficial to readers in search of entertainment within the limited time frame of their daily activities. Most of the stories will bring back fond memories to the African and Caribbean diaspora as the settings range across Canada, France, Ghana, Jamaica, Kenya, Liberia, Nigeria, Sierra Leone, The Gambia and United Kingdom. In a bid to defy death, this book is written primarily for posterity. Folks from Sierra Leone, a country that was once hailed as the *Athens of West Africa* in terms of enlightenment will see themselves once more taking their rightful place in the realm of African Literature.

My heartfelt thanks for support and encouragement in writing this book go to: Mariama Mansaray of Ottawa and Irene Brown of Edmonton, both in Canada, for reminding me of the simple pleasures in life; Efioanwan Fifi Edem for the editorial service; Aruna Deen Stro of Blackpool, United Kingdom for the illustrations; and the team at PageMaster Publication Services Inc. for their craftsmanship.

I wish to thank my family, relatives and friends whose presence in my life I appreciate enormously.

Bakar Mansaray
July 2015

Online Dating Comes To Accra

"Hi, care for a chat?" Black Prince wrote in small green Arial font.

"Sure," Ebony Princess wrote back in 12-point type black Times New Roman font.

"How are you?" read the next sentence from Black Prince.

"Fine, thank you. And you?" Ebony Princess responded and then switched on her bedside lamp.

"Apart from London's cold weather, I can't complain," wrote Black Prince.

"So, what are you looking for on this dating site?" wrote Ebony Princess.

"I'm looking for someone to become my wife. And you?"

"I'm looking for a potential husband."

"Well, that's good."

"Where are you from, Black Prince?"

"Ghana," he replied.

"Oh, that's interesting, I'm from Ghana too."

"What's your name, Ebony Princess?"

"Afua is my name."

"Wow, so both of us were born on a Friday!"

"What do you mean?"

"Call me Kofi. I'm from the Akan tribe too."

"This sounds interesting," she wrote, blinking her eyes.

"I've to tell you something, though," he wrote.

"Before you say it, can we please chat via Skype instead?" she wrote back.

"Ok," Kofi agreed.

They exchanged Skype addresses and within minutes Afua and Kofi could see each other via web camera on the screen of their computers. Afua was in her bedroom in Accra, Ghana and Kofi was in his study in London, England. While she looked gorgeous but unsettled in her apple-red silk night-gown, Kofi, a tall, slim and charming looking man was more relaxed in his favourite yellow Tee-shirt and blue jeans.

"Now, what was it you wanted to tell me?" Afua asked.

"I'm really fifty-one," said Kofi.

Afua's eyes opened wide. "You look younger than your age."

"Thank you," he laughed.

"How come you lied in your online profile?" she asked.

"Because I was afraid nobody will contact me."

"I see." She nodded slowly, admiring Kofi's frankness.

She reached for a glass of water and with the other hand she fidgeted with her head tie, a matching apple-red silk. Afua was an attractive woman: average height, full-figured, and graceful looking. She almost always wore a smile. Kofi couldn't take his eyes off her. He admired her beauty as she fanned her face with a colourful hand-held Japanese fan.

"It must be hot out there," he said.

"Yes, it is," she giggled.

"For how long have you been separated from your husband?" he asked.

"One year," she lied.

"I'm sorry to hear that," he told her.

"Oh, that's ok," she replied, staring blankly at Kofi, wondering if he could read her mind.

A few weeks ago, Afua's life was in shambles. That was when she subscribed as a non-paying member to AfroIntroductions.com, an African dating website for singles. Her husband of three years, Agymah, had just left their childless marriage for another woman, days before her thirty-ninth birthday. The other woman was, he had claimed, his business partner. She had visited them on a couple of occasions. How did she not see this coming? She wondered. Suddenly, the stakes had become higher for her. Firstly, age was not on her side, and secondly, she had no children to console her. The thought of having to start over again made her nauseated. For her, spending long hours on the dating website was a form of escape. How was she to find someone who fully understood her? Baffled and without an answer, she was no longer sleeping properly at night.

"So what do you do for a living?" Kofi continued.

"I've been married to my job as a Sales Executive for a mobile telephone firm," she replied.

"Married to your job," he repeated, glancing at her in disbelief. "Maybe that was why the guy left you."

"Maybe," she muttered.

"And, like me, Afua, you prefer online dating?"

"Not really, but it isn't easy meeting people."

"For an isolated single man like me, the dating website serves as a springboard."

"I had quite a few friends who set me on blind dates. None of them ever worked out," she said.

"For me, going on the Internet was less scary than meeting women in person."

"Are you scared of women?"

"No, but online, you've more options of picking and choosing without hurting anybody's feelings."

"I'm planning to leave Ghana for Europe, Canada or the U.S."

"Come to England then."

"That's fine," she said smiling.

"Aren't you afraid to meet a stranger?"

"It depends. And you're my country man."

But Kofi was right, Afua thought. She had heard of people getting themselves killed by strangers posing as friends on the Internet. They met someone on the Internet and ended up dead or in foreign lands as sex slaves.

"If you like I can contact a guy who is running an immigration consultancy out here."

"Please do and let me know his terms," Afua consented.

Within the next couple of days they exchanged telephone numbers and flirted insanely. Kofi sent her the web link of a London-based immigration consultancy that was asking for £300 as an initial fee. They claimed to ease their client's immigration burden by making a strong case on their behalf and by gathering evidence and developing a convincing presentation of their cases. Kofi promised to settle half of the fee if she could remit the remaining amount to his cousin in Accra.

As Afua could not make up her mind on the whole deal, she invited her girlfriend, Agbenyaga, for lunch at Accra's La Palm Royal Beach Hotel restaurant. Afua trusted her advice, especially with Agymah gone and Kofi trying to seduce her. The sound of Agbenyaga's warm voice always comforted her. However, although Agbenyaga was an inspiration to Afua in so many ways, she had not been able to stand

Agbenyaga's romantic insinuations. Every now and then she would ask Afua for a kiss, a cuddle, and even at one time, sex. Agbenyaga, in her attempts to seduce her always pointed out that men were not worth a pinch of salt these days. If she, Agbenyaga, could do without men and children, why couldn't Afua? As far as she was concerned, men were two a penny and children could be adopted.

Agbenyaga was tall and slim, with short black hair and dark, crystalline eyes. She was in good health, single, no children, and a banker by profession — a senior executive at the Borkor Commercial Bank Limited. When she learnt from Afua that she was on a dating website, she acknowledged the news with a condescending sneer. She mentioned how such websites were full of creepy weird folks.

Hence, once they sat down together for lunch, Agbenyaga asked, "Have you met your Waterloo?"

"My notable and decisive defeat is yet to come," replied Afua.

"So what's up then, Afua?"

She explained to Agbenyaga about Kofi's proposal and her part in the payment of the immigration consultant's fee.

"There you go, another scam in the making," said Agbenyaga.

"But this fellow sounded genuine," countered Afua.

"Can't you see that his offer of a partial payment is bait? I wouldn't trust him," Agbenyaga waved her hand dismissively.

"But Agbenyaga . . ."

"Listen, men don't like to be chased," said Agbenyaga, with a sneer "You've got to grow up, Afua."

In the next several weeks, she continued to get grief from Agbenyaga, whose advice fell on deaf ears. Afua did not realize how serious her relationship with Kofi was getting. For her, it just felt right. As she was starting to fall in love with him, she gave £150 to Kofi's cousin, a fellow by the name of Mensah.

Then everything changed. Kofi could neither be seen online nor heard on the telephone anymore. Afua made several desperate attempts to reach him and Mensah but to no avail. In her state of confusion, she could not muster the courage to inform Agbenyaga about her defeat. She regretted not having taken more time to get to know

Kofi first. She became morose and lonely, although not for too long. She went back to online dating.

✖ ✖ ✖

By using the same website, AfroIntroductions.com, Afua decided to date Caucasian men only. She had concluded that the Black men were not to be trusted. She was now even more determined to leave the country than before. Whenever Agbenyaga asked her about her exploits, she would coyly dismiss the topic.

One day, no sooner had she logged online than a Caucasian man approached her for a chat. Apparently, both his online and real name were Ted. He claimed to be an Australian working as a mining engineer for the Asap Vasa II Gold Refinery Company Limited in Ghana. After some intensive flirting he asked Afua to write a brief story about herself, and to submit her Curriculum Vitae to him. He hinted that he may sponsor her to emigrate from Ghana to Australia or find her a lucrative job in Ghana's gold mining industry.

Until he requested for cybersex, Afua counted herself lucky to have met such a handsome, well-built man who was in his mid-fifties. But she did not want to refuse his request for fear of losing his goodwill. For several days in a row they would exhibit their nudity online, masturbate, and exchange their nude photographs. Although Ted was clearly enjoying their erotic thrills, Afua felt embarrassed and cheap.

"I would prefer we meet in person rather than being nude online," she suggested.

"That's absolutely fine with me," he promptly accepted.

"When and where would you like us to meet?" she asked.

"You know what? Send me that CV and the brief story about yourself and we'll take it from there."

"All right," Afua agreed and wrote the following lines to Ted:

Driven by a desire to escape the poverty that plagued my unemployed parents, and coupled with my ambition to be financially stable, I will always remember the month of June 1991. It will always be a time in my life that signified economic transformation. At the age of 21, a year before I completed my tertiary education at the University of Ghana, I resorted to selling fashionable tissue boxes. By then, I also worked as a research assistant when on vacation. I did not make much profit as I was buying them in Accra and selling them in areas where we participated in agricultural shows. Within a short time I realized how thrifty I was. By saving most of my business capital and not living a luxurious life, I had a good sum saved up.

When University reopened, an acquaintance told me how a friend of hers was selling clothing items imported from Abidjan. I approached the lady and asked her to take me along on her trip to Abidjan. The currency exchange rate between the Cedi and the CFA then was relatively good.

My first trip to Abidjan was with two couples and I was the rookie among them. We rented a car which was driven by my friend's boyfriend. The trip went well and I had with me only $500. With this amount I was able to buy typical casual clothes for university students. The goods sold like hot cakes and I had to get some more that same semester because the demand was high. A third visit was planned but unfortunately it was a holiday, hence we could only buy from flea markets.

During my final year of schooling, I sold more and saved a lot. My love of this type of business was coupled with my love for travelling. Plateau, downtown Abidjan then, was the place to be. The glitz and sophisticated nightlife was found down town. I started including beddings in my consignment. I attracted older people as my clientele. My sister-in-law realized that I was focused, so she once took me along when travelling to Lome, Togo, on a business venture. That trip also was profitable.

In the year 1994, I travelled to Lagos, Nigeria, on a package holiday. I was wise enough to take part of my business capital to purchase goods. I discovered a chain of factory shops not very far from where we were accommodated. I travelled back to the same place in 1998 after an acquaintance told me of a place that sold nice fashionable shoes. I brought back to Ghana some of these shoes, which sold well. The main problem with the Lagos trips was that I travelled by road for a couple of days. Although the coaches were luxurious, the trip was too long. I literally slept the whole night.

In the year 2004, the Government of India awarded me a scholarship to study for a one year programme in Delhi. This was a breakthrough for me professionally and business-wise. I discovered that Indians were good at making things with their hands. I started importing handmade hand bags and leather jackets. The issue was that I could not interact with my customers, but had to get a middle man to do that for me.

I had now settled in India, although the conditions were unbearable; the meals, the pollution and over-population left much to be desired. We were about 40 kilometres from the city centre but it took us two hours to reach Delhi mainly because of the bumper-to-bumper traffic jam. The place was called Narela, a sub city in the Delhi area. The study program was very hectic. It was mainly held for Africans, Asians, and students from the Caribbean Islands and the Pacific. We were all from developing countries. There were no Indian students.

There were six of us from Ghana, five being men from the Ghana Defence Force, and myself. Four of them were doing Advanced Diplomas and one was doing a Masters. Since this was a Hindi society, it took me some time to locate a Christian place of worship. It was a very small group and it took place in somebody's house.

On completion of my studies, beginning of the year 2005, I started my business in flea markets. This I did for some time. The main problem with selling at flea markets was that I didn't have a van then to transport my wares. At the end of 2007, I stopped going to the flea markets and sold from home. It has been five years now and my small business has grown. I have my clientele.

My business had challenges as I sold on credit most of the time. I met unscrupulous characters who took the goods and disappeared or the stubborn ones who didn't even pay after several reminders. I didn't have overheads as I was the one who sold and did everything from my house. I aimed to open chain stores selling fashionable items in town. Most people imported from China, I would like to explore Vietnam, Guatemala and Indonesia.

Impressed by Afua's ambitious character, Ted invited her for dinner at the Golden Tulip Hotel restaurant on Liberation Road. On the night of their date, he was courteous and well- mannered.

He held the restaurant door open for her, spoke nicely to her and the restaurant staff. He encouraged Afua to try a particular vintage red wine, three appetizers, and a grilled Ghanaian sea bass special as main course. By the end of dinner, she found Ted not only humorous and interesting but also generous and able to maintain a decent conversation. He slipped a hundred dollar bill into the breast pocket of her blouse and insisted on giving her a ride home. Once at her residence, he asked if he could enter the house.

"You're a beauty, baby," he said as they shuffled into her bedroom.

Although she was unprepared to receive a guest that late in the night, she thawed under his compliments. It was slowly dawning on her that she may not be able to resist his seduction. Then it all started as quickly as a flash of lightning. Ted looked at Afua in a certain way, with a certain intent. She returned his look, eyes caressing him.

"Isn't it an unusually hot night?" she winked coquettishly at him and switched on the table fan.

"It is, my dear", replied Ted whose shirt was now sodden and tightly clung to his back.

Afua then turned on the stereo and the slow, soft music of Aretha Franklin, *Until You Say You Love Me*, filled the air. She went into her bathroom and when she returned to the bedroom, Ted's breath caught in his throat. He liked to think that because his childhood was spent in a family of women, he had developed a love for women. And they loved him, both young and old. He spared none. Even the wives of his friends, prostitutes and the like. Afua was now in bed, eyes closed. Her mind slipped into solitude. As the air from the fan embraced her naked body, the memories of the time spent together with Ted in the restaurant filled her head. She smiled and glanced in the mirror across from the bed. Her skin glowed from her body heat. Reaching for the light switch, she turned off the main lights. The bedroom remained dimly lit by a smaller lamp.

Resting her hand on her stomach, the heat exploded from her body. She sucked her index finger, taking in a deep breath, exhaling slowly and relaxing into the mood that was engulfing her. Ted whispered to her, telling her what to do. She responded to his bidding. At first, she was self-conscious, but now, the exhibitionist comes alive. She has fallen into his clutches, he muses. He sat back looking at her with pleasure in his smile. When he murmured his approval, she continued to caress herself. In less than thirty minutes, the erotic show ended as abruptly as it started. Ted kissed her goodbye and she was left yearning for a husband and not just a date.

In the days that followed, Afua and Ted continued to flirt online and by telephone. He encouraged Afua to complete an application form for permanent residency in Australia. He paid the application fees and the express courier service charges. And then shortly after, he told Afua over the telephone that he was leaving Ghana for good.

"Why are you leaving so unceremoniously?" she asked.

"I've become a victim of circumstance at my workplace," he replied.

"I'm so sorry to hear that," she said.

"Keep me posted on your immigration application process," he said, and the telephone went dead.

It was only later Afua learnt that Ted was forced to resign from his job because he had an affair with the wife of his boss.

✕ ✕ ✕

Although online dating had not made it easier for Afua to get a husband, she continued to visit the dating website. As a marketing strategy, she purchased a one month membership subscription for about $30. She had the impression that she now knew exactly who she was looking for, and she was determined to go out with more men with a view to increase the probability of finding a Mr. Right. Perseverance, she believed, could pay a worthwhile dividend if one was lucky. When asked by her friend, Agbenyaga, if all was well, she would reply in the affirmative. She had come to terms with the fact that she had neither seen nor heard from her husband, Agymah, since he eloped with another woman.

One evening, Afua returned home from work feeling good. After having a light supper of cheeseburger and chocolate drink, she turned on her computer and logged in to the dating website. She clicked into iTunes and momentarily Bob Marley's *Trenchtown Rock* filled the air. He sang, *"One good thing about music, when it hits you, you feel no pain."* Afua sat back in her chair and drank some iced water, staring at the profiles of men in the United States.

His username was Simba Imani and his profile photo captivated her. He was smiling a knowing smile and his eyes bored right through her and beyond. Afua thought that he looked confident and at ease with himself. His facial features were carefully chiseled like that of a Fulani; dark in complexion, supple and gracefully handsome. Another photo in his gallery showed him standing in Accra's Independence Square with the Independence Arch monument in the background. The large black star and the inscriptions *A.D. 1957, Freedom and Justice,* could be vividly seen. This photo made Afua become more interested in Simba Imani.

According to his profile data, he was five feet eight tall, an American of Kenyan descent, and a non-smoker who drank occasionally. His marital status was single. He worked as a financial advisor for an insurance firm in New Jersey.

Afua heard a *ping* and almost leaped out of her seat. It was Simba Imani! He must have noticed that she, Ebony Princess, was browsing through his profile data. He wanted to chat!

SIMBA IMANI: Hi! Can you spare a couple of minutes?

EBONY PRINCESS: Hi! Sure

SIMBA IMANI: I was in Accra on a business trip two years ago.

EBONY PRINCESS: Really?

SIMBA IMANI: Yeah. Haven't you seen my photo, taken at the Independence Square?

EBONY PRINCESS: I saw it but I thought it was one of those superimposed photos

SIMBA IMANI: Come on. Why would you think that way?

EBONY PRINCESS: I don't know. What's your real name?

SIMBA IMANI: Simba Imani, meaning Lion Faith in Swahili.

EBONY PRINCESS: Are you a Muslim? And are you single?

SIMBA IMANI: Yeah, a non-religious one. I'm single.

EBONY PRINCESS: Okay. Now I see why your profile says that you drink occasionally. So, what are you looking for on this dating site?

SIMBA IMANI: A potential wife who would be able to meet me in New Jersey.

EBONY PRINCESS: It's not that easy, you know.

SIMBA IMANI: I know but I'm ready to sponsor that person.

EBONY PRINCESS: Who would that lucky person be in a world where women out-number men?

SIMBA IMANI: It could be even you, though good husbands are hard to come by. It's rather pathetic about this one man, one wife thing. Nature didn't mean it to be so.

EBONY PRINCESS: Meaning we should give up as women and just share the men? In Ghana, the ratio of women to men stands at 52:48. So, if I really want to keep you here, I have to provide and take care of you like a baby. Women are hard working here and most of them are single parents. If you have to join me in Accra, I'll have to be extra careful as women will snatch you under my nose. LOL

SIMBA IMANI: But this is a common ratio world-wide. It makes some men lazy and dependent on women. Men, though, should be hard-working if they are to keep more than one wife.

For many days after, Afua and Simba Imani chatted and flirted online. They made telephone calls to each other. She concluded that even though they were not totally compatible she was going to give the relationship a try. Moreover, when she looked at people she knew who were in relationships; none of them seemed to be well-matched. So, Afua started making plans to visit Simba Imani in the United States, especially when one day he said, "I want to marry you."

"You must be joking," she told him.

"I'm not joking," he said.

"I hope that you're not playing with my affection for you."

"Why should I, Afua?"

She had a tough time sleeping that night. During the lengthy Skype telephone calls, mostly initiated by Simba Imani, she had a vivid picture of his apartment. From the webcam, she discovered that the decoration was simple, reflecting a man's environment. However, it had all the basic things to make her feel comfortable. She pictured herself in the apartment one day when funds and time permitted, and longed for it to be soon.

She could not take him off her mind, for the last conversation had sweet words of assurance of being loved. Once in a while, it dawned on her that this was only a long distance relationship and hence she should not be carried away. The sweet part of it was that someone out there cared about her. During one of her office meetings, she could not help it but exchanged series of text messages to him using her cell phone.

Afua wanted to spend the festive Christmas season with someone she really loved. She thought Simba Imani was a perfect candidate. At times, she thought that he was playing on her intelligence. She suspected that he was a married man who claimed to be single. Dumping all reasoning, she applied for a visitor's visa, paid her airfare, and travelled to the United States to meet Simba Imani.

She was expecting him to meet her at the airport, but there was no Simba Imani to be seen. She reached for a public telephone and dialled his number.

"I'm sorry but I'm busy now," he said.

"Hello Simba Imani! This is Afua. I'm waiting at the airport."

"Can you find an airport hotel to stay for now? I'll foot the bill." The words were lost on her.

Afua heard the voice of a woman talking to a child in the background.

"But you said . . ." Then the telephone line went dead. A lump of anger rose in her throat. Feeling like a heel, she drew in sharp angry breaths. Dimly, she realized that something new was happening in her world. Tears veiled her eyes. She broke into hysterics and there was no holding her now. Passersby turned and stared at her. A uniformed female airport attendant walked up to Afua and asked if she could be of help.

"How do I get to the nearest hotel?" She asked the attendant, her lip curled in disgust.

"By taxi cab, The Sheraton will be your best choice."

Once she settled down in the hotel, all the tales she had heard about online dating came crowding back. She began to realize why Simba Imani was at times rather cagey in his approach. She wondered why her honesty to him had only been rewarded by deceitfulness. She swallowed her grief, anger and disappointment and dialed his telephone number again. To her dismay, an automated voice said that the number was no longer in service. Stars burst before her eyes. A tear drop ran down her cheek, she licked it up and started sobbing afresh. Her eyes were now sunken from lack of sleep and misery. She yawned and again pondered her foolishness.

The next day, Afua gave her friend, Agbenyaga, a telephone call hoping to find someone to console her.

"I'm sorry Afua, but your behaviour is unbelievable," she cried out.

"I know. He played on my love for him."

"Come on. How can you love someone just like that?"

"Agbenyaga, you know the weakness of women."

"But not to such an extent, my friend."

"I feel deep sympathy and sorrow for myself and women seeking husbands online."

"You don't need to Afua. They asked for it."

"I'll never trust any man again."

That same day, Afua received an email from Ted, the Australian mining engineer, asking for her hand in marriage. She sucked her teeth in irritation and wrote to him saying no to his proposal. Within the next couple of days, Afua changed her return flight reservation and headed back to Accra. Upon her arrival home, Agymah, her husband was waiting for her.

"I'm sorry, Afua please forgive me," he said, kneeling down in front of her. He could feel sweat dripping from his armpits as he waited anxiously to hear Afua's response. She had to stifle a sudden urge to laugh as she felt a strange tide of satisfaction.

"Agymah, you're my husband. I've nothing against you."

"Thank you, Afua. I'm just another prodigal husband."

She sucked her teeth, shook her head and smiled, saying "Oh you men."

2

Virginia's Triple Cocktail

"You're HIV positive, my dear." Dr. Jacob Kamara's solemn voice resounded through the clinic's consultation room.

Virginia froze in her seat. "But last year's test showed negative," she murmured, as her heart skipped a beat.

"It doesn't matter," replied the doctor.

"I can't see how . . ." she began to say but her heart raced so fast she could hardly speak. Panic sweat broke out on her forehead even though the room was air-conditioned. Her clasped hands, stiff as borax, were supported by the doctor's desk. She felt as frightened as a rabbit among a pack of dogs. She stood up. Her eyes caught her own reflection in a mirror hanging on the wall. Her dark complexion had become even darker. The brightly-coloured cotton blouse and blue jeans she wore had been neat once; now they looked ruffled and untidy.

For a moment she felt her forehead and realized her temperature was going up. She rubbed her neck, which featured a tattoo of the monarch butterfly. It meant something to her, that tattoo. But it could not hold her attention long. She gazed at her own image with much wonder. A short, full-figured woman just into her late twenties, she had been beautiful once. But now her hair was unkempt and her face lined and strained by worry. Her dark eyes had seen too much. She took a quick glance at the doctor and burst into tears.

"Help me, doctor, please help me!" she cried, begging for what she knew she could not possibly receive.

"Tell me, how have you been feeling lately?" Dr. Kamara asked.

"Unwell. Headaches, runny nose, frequent sore throat and fatigue," replied Virginia.

"Have you noticed any weight loss and rashes?"

Just the mention of rashes brought prickly hives to her skin. "Yes," she replied. Her eyes widened, darted wildly like a trapped animal, then back to the doctor.

"I'll get you to do a confirmatory test in order to determine your viral count," said Dr. Kamara.

She nodded her head nervously in response and left the room to do the test in an adjoining laboratory.

She remembered the last conversation that she had with her mother, before she passed away. Lying down on her death bed, she insisted on confessing to Virginia.

"You'll have to forgive me, my daughter," said her mother.

"I forgive you for whatever it is, but don't tell me," said Virginia.

"I need to tell you so I can die peacefully."

"Well, if you insist then go ahead."

"Your uncle Ben is your biological father," said her mother, sobbing uncontrollably.

"What do you mean, Mama?" Virginia asked in a hoarse voice.

"I had an affair with your uncle when your father was a political prisoner. He died in prison," her mother added.

"That's enough, Mama," cried Virginia.

"Please forgive me, my daughter."

"I forgive you, Mama," said Virginia, holding on to her mother's hands until she passed away.

After the death of her mother, Virginia was forced to quit high school, as none of her relatives could afford to pay her school fees. A man called Samson introduced her to prostitution. As she thought about her life story, Virginia's thoughts became overwhelmingly suicidal.

⚔ ⚔ ⚔

A couple of days later Virginia consulted Dr. Kamara again.

"I'm sorry to say, but the confirmatory test shows that you're HIV positive," said the doctor.

Virginia looked directly at the doctor, extended her arms and said, "Hold my hands."

Although Dr. Kamara was slightly taken aback by the request, he reached out and held her hands briefly before letting go again.

Then she burst out laughing. She laughed so hard tears ran down her cheeks. She gave Dr. Kamara a hug and a kiss on the cheek.

"I love you, doctor," she said.

Gently, the doctor pushed her away, smiling in astonishment.

"You should be fine, Virginia, as the infection is still in its early stages." He waited to see Virginia's reaction.

"Am I going to die, doctor?" she asked, with tears but not fear in her eyes.

"We'll all die one day," replied the doctor.

"But when will this disease kill me?"

"I can't tell, my dear. All I can say for now is that you wouldn't be placed on antiretroviral drugs because your viral load is still low."

"Does that mean I will survive?"

"Yes, you will if you take the prescribed drugs."

"I believe you, Dr. Kamara. I believe you," she said hysterically.

"Well, the treatment will start with three different drugs — the triple cocktail, we call it. You'll also need regular counselling," concluded the doctor, as if passing a sentence.

Even though the doctor appeared to be quite calm, Virginia felt that this diagnosis was going to be the harbinger of darkness in her life. She wondered when and how she had been infected by the disease. Could it have been Samson, her pimp-cum-lover or was it someone else? Would the medications improve her health, she asked herself?

Virginia joined Samson who was waiting for her at the clinic's reception desk. When he saw her solemn countenance, he jumped from his seat, stepping too lightly for a man of his stature, which was nearly twice that of Virginia. A forced smile split his thick lips and his broad face which was topped by short black curly hair that sat on his head like a hat. His faded brown Tee-shirt hugged his muscular frame so tightly that he looked like a teenager even though he was in his mid-thirties. His baggy khaki shorts were held in place by a worn-out leather belt. The rubber sandals on his feet looked as if they badly needed a cobbler's attention. Virginia started to cry as though her tears would overturn the mind-twisting news she had just received. She shivered with the memory.

"What's wrong?" he asked.

She sighed deeply. "Nothing," she replied, although she knew a lot was wrong. Virginia was not so sure whether to break the news to Samson or not. She feared that he might abandon her. But who else would console and help her besides Samson and the doctor? Would Mama Ehga, her boss at *Paradise on Earth*, allow her to stay and ply her trade at the brothel? Virginia was yet to explain to Mama Ehga how she had lost one of the brothel's most influential clients—a senior officer in the military just a few days ago. She risked getting fired. To add salt to injury, she would also have to contend with the societal stigma associated with HIV and AIDS.

"Come on, Virginia, what did the doctor say?" Samson asked impatiently.

"I'm HIV positive," she said simply, and he flinched as she added, "the doctor said all will be well." Her voice stretched in irony.

"What did you say?" he asked.

"Positive . . . I'm HIV positive," she repeated as if there was a period between each word.

"I'm sorry to hear this, Virginia," Samson said, wondering if he was also carrying the deadly virus. He hugged her tight for some time and then let go.

"I need to get the drugs from the government pharmacy," she said.

"I'll go with you," he volunteered, leading the way. They left the clinic with Samson's arm around her shoulder.

❆ ❆ ❆

Checkered rays of sunlight cast through dark clouds as the rains poured over drought-stricken Freetown like manna from heaven. Born in the great Atlantic Ocean, the wind blew east, beating at everything. Motorists cursed in mad annoyance at potholes and honked their horns unnecessarily. The streets were almost deserted except for few pedestrians like Virginia and Samson who were manoeuvring through ankle-deep pools of reddish-brown water. His rainbow-coloured umbrella barely covered her wide rolling hips, let alone his frame. Samson managed a faint smile. Of all things he would have wanted to think about right now, Virginia's hips was way down the list. No, he did not want to add that to his thoughts.

He checked his watch. They only had fifteen minutes to get to the pharmacy. He was worried that it might be closing early because of bad weather.

"I'm tired," she said, shivering and coughing.

"Come on, we're almost there," Samson urged her.

At the pharmacy, dozens of people queued up patiently for their turn to be attended to by a knot of sluggish attendants behind a counter. A small group of Jehovah's Witnesses engaged a couple of people in brief conversations in the slow-moving queue. One of the ladies in the group of Jehovah's Witnesses walked up to Virginia and greeted her.

"Your face looks familiar to me," she said.

"I don't remember meeting you before," Virginia lied. She had seen the lady before at Mama Ehga's brothel.

"Oh, that's fine. I may be wrong," said the Jehovah's Witness.

Virginia turned towards Samson in order to avoid the lady. But he was engaged in conversation with some other people.

"I would like to invite you for prayers at our church," the lady said smiling and giving Virginia a flyer.

"Thank you, I'll give you a call when I'm ready," said Virginia, touching her forehead again and realizing that her temperature had risen further. It seemed as if the ceiling fan in the pharmacy was blowing all the room's hot air upon her.

Samson had now finished conversing with the other people. He stood quietly by Virginia's side like a stone in the midst of a drifting dream. She became lost in her thoughts; oblivious of her cacophonous surroundings save for the smell of medicines that kept her nose twitching.

By now, they were at the head of the queue facing a sullen female employee who demanded, "How can I help you?"

Virginia gave her the prescription from the doctor. The employee gave it a quick glance and shoved it back at Virginia, querying, "But why should Dr. Kamara prescribe such a large quantity of drugs for one person?" She carried the expression of a woman who thought herself better than those around her. Virginia was speechless. She rubbed her cheek briskly, wondering what to say.

Samson replied, "We don't know . . . "

"I'm not talking to you, Mister," the employee almost shouted.

Virginia and Samson were both taken aback, not knowing what next to say or do.

"You have to pay a quarter of the cost," said the employee with elaborate casualness.

"I thought the drugs were free," Virginia ventured in a hushed tone.

"Free where? You mean in this country?" The employee smiled, her mouth twisting briefly with distaste.

"I can't believe this." Virginia shuddered and raised a hand as though to ward off something.

"You have to pay for cost recovery," said the employee.

"What does that mean?" Virginia asked.

"Administrative cost."

"Who said so?"

"I said so," replied the employee arrogantly.

"No, you can't, what you want is a bribe."

The employee gave Virginia a nasty look. "No wonder you're HIV positive," she remarked, followed by a long hiss.

Virginia felt defeated. "That's none of your business," she said knowing fully well that she must now be ready to contend with the societal stigma associated with HIV and AIDS.

"I don't care," the employee replied dismissively.

Virginia and Samson left the pharmacy, walking back into the rain without the drugs. They felt like rats swimming upstream in uncharted waters. Virginia entertained a flicker of hope that she would be able to talk herself out of the mess which losing an influential client had put her. Maybe she could even get a loan from Mama Ehga if she wasn't fired first.

✂ ✂ ✂

The weather the next day was sunny and yet humid. Virginia tried to explain to Mama Ehga how she lost the brothel's influential client but when her eyes met Mama Ehga, she could only stare silently in fear. Mama Ehga was known for her temper. She flared up at everything. It was difficult to put any age on her but she could have been in her early fifties. There was a maturity in her large, dark eyes which did not quite match her cherubic face. For a moment, Virginia felt those eyes on her like deep lakes about to drown her.

Mama Ehga carried herself with an air of authority, exhibiting an aura of superiority and arrogance that always made people feel restless. She was a couple of degrees shy of being obese and stood at nearly six feet tall. A black lace veil framed her face and her black hair, hung down in braids. For the past two years or so in which Virginia had known her, she always wore a black flowing gown. She was said to be mourning the death of her husband who had died in a ship fire. Her left hand had rings on all five fingers. Mama Ehga sat in a red velvet rocking chair flanked by two of her chaperones.

"Yes, Queen Virginia, what happened between you and my client?" Mama Ehga demanded in a clear voice. Her mouth, outlined by her trademark black lipstick, was small for a woman of her size.

"He forced himself on me without a condom . . ."

"And so what happened?"

Virginia paused. "I slapped him on the face."

"You did what?" Mama Ehga fumed, her breath whistling out of her nostrils.

"I was . . ."

"He told me that you called him every sort of nasty name."

"No, I didn't," said Virginia, as a flush drained her body of strength, like blood drained through a tube.

"You're in danger, Virginia!" The words sounded like a threat.

"What?"

"That client is a senior officer in the military, and he is ready to take revenge."

"Please, Madam, tell him that I'm sorry. I have enough problems."

"I don't know, but he was terribly mad at you."

"See what I mean," said Virginia, showing her the medical prescription.

"What's this?" asked Mama Ehga disdainfully.

"Please loan me some money to buy these drugs."

"What's wrong with you?"

"I'm not well," said Virginia, too shy to disclose her health status.

"We've lost an influential client because of you and you've the guts to demand money from me?"

"I'm sorry, Madam . . ." Virginia tried to mutter a plea.

"Get out of my sight!" shouted Mama Ehga. "Never step your feet here again," she added, standing up as if ready to pounce.

The brothel had been home to Virginia for more than two years. The incessant chatter of the girls was music in her ears. To be banished from it was a shock. She looked at Mama Ehga in that intense, consuming manner that reflected hate and malice. She wanted to devour her flesh like a vulture on a carcass. But she accepted her fate and walked away.

⚜ ⚜ ⚜

Virginia took a deep breath, thinking about Mama Ehga and the sullen female employee at the pharmacy. These two women, she thought, had contributed to making her life miserable. She blamed herself for sleeping with strange men unprotected. Now that her hope of gaining sympathy from Mama Ehga had flown out the window, Virginia had the urge to visit her relatives.

"No," she said out loud, wiping sweat from her forehead, "not my relatives." They had shunned her long ago when she took to the streets. For now, Samson would be her salvation. His words were like sparkles, hovering around her, and gliding away sky-high. Visions of him danced in her mind every time she closed her eyes.

Later that evening she met Samson in a dilapidated three-bedroom wooden shack that he shared with some other tenants in a neighbourhood called Katakoumbay, one of Freetown's infamous prostitutes' enclaves. The place was a fishing hamlet located down a cliff along the seaside. It was infested with flies during the day and mosquitoes at night. The infestation was made worse by the hot and humid weather. Piracy, gambling, over-crowding, noise, and drug abuse were endemic in the community.

"How did it go?" Samson demanded, making no effort to hide his anxiety. "I've been waiting for you to have lunch."

Virginia stared at her friend in disillusionment. "She fired me without any money," she answered calmly.

"So what did you tell her?"

Virginia recounted her visit to Mama Ehga, watching for signs of emotion in him. But Samson's face gave nothing away. His blazing dark eyes remained fixed on Virginia's full figure as she spoke. Virginia's broad hips always mesmerized him.

"What are you staring at?" She asked, suddenly aware of Samson's gaze.

"You look sweet," he said.

"Thank you, but what next?" she enquired, softening under his flattery.

"I've some good news for you but before then come here," he said with a smile. There was a sincerity to his smile that moved her.

He shoved her gently onto the rickety bed.

"No, Samson, please don't."

The blood in Samson rushed through him, defying Virginia's plea. The drive to sleep with her became more energized.

He reached for a condom. He placed his hands under her and pulled her to him. There wasn't a questioning look. They understood their needs. He carelessly allowed his hands to run down over her stomach and between her aching, swollen loins. He then traced his finger over her cheek and then her lips. Virginia took a deep breath as she felt a shiver run through her. She could not suppress a few groans. Ecstasy enveloped them as they surrendered their bodies to those blissful yearnings. And what seemed ages was actually a matter of minutes. Both of them lay down side by side exhausted.

"Now that you've got what you want, tell me the good news," demanded Virginia of a beaming Samson.

He rummaged in his shirt pocket and came out with a piece of paper, saying excitedly, "I registered your name for medical treatment."

"Where did you do that?" Virginia reacted as if she has heard a story stranger than fiction.

"I did that at the head of the community's compound."

"Why there?"

"A mobile health unit will visit the community in the morning".

"What will it cost?" She asked anxiously.

"It'll be free of charge," he said with a broad smile.

"Ah," she breathed with satisfaction. Like someone in a dream world, she added, "that's so nice of you, Samson."

"It's my duty, Virginia" he said with satisfaction.

The wind blew and the curtain billowed into the room, and she moved to the window. A radiant flash of lightning lit up the dull and gloomy sky, followed by a thunder clap and pattering rain.

"Bedtime, Virginia," Samson called out. Her name on his lips sounded melodious. Samson was one of the few people who had ever cared for her, she mused as she fell asleep in his arms.

But her dreams that night were troubling. She dreamt that she was carrying a coffin. A military man appeared in the dream asking her where she was going. She told him that she was relocating to another cemetery because she did not like where she was buried. The military man took to his heels in a flash. She woke up in the middle of the night sweating profusely.

✣ ✣ ✣

"Can I have your attention please?" a male health worker shouted to the small crowd that had lined up for treatment. An eerie silence followed, enveloped in blistering hot air. The mobile health unit, like Virginia and Samson, had been at the compound of the head of the community since sunrise. Both lovers were in front of the queue. A temporary tent, with the words *Médecins sans Frontières* written on it, had been erected in the compound for the purpose of a triage.

"We'll do HIV, TB, and pregnancy tests for the first twenty women," the health worker said, taking a sweeping look across the crowd, and then at his colleagues. "The first fifteen men will take tests for HIV and TB," he continued as the crowd murmured. "We'll provide you with the necessary drugs, free of charge." On hearing this, Virginia smiled at Samson. By the look of things, she thought, it seemed as if these folks were not going to ignore her like furniture. Due to fear of the unknown, she was worried about the idea of doing TB and pregnancy tests. Why would she want to open a Pandora's Box when all seemed well, she asked herself. She said a little prayer of thanks and waited with hope until she was called into the tent for the tests. After a long wait, she was invited for consultation with a doctor.

A female Caucasian doctor took a quick glance at Virginia and shook her head.

"Are you a mother with children?" asked the doctor.

The question sent bile rushing into her mouth. She looked as if she was going to faint. Fear threatened to choke her as she shook. This is it, she thought. She might be pregnant.

"The tests showed that you're HIV positive."

"I know, so all I need now is treatment," she said with calm.

"You may also need some counselling," said the doctor, taken aback by Virginia's confident attitude.

"That's fine with me," she replied.

From the prescription, it was obvious that Virginia had to follow a strict regimen. It was the combination of drugs that struck her. She dreaded the dosage and size of the pills, as they made her feel nauseous. The doctor warned that lack of adherence would cause viral resistance.

Virginia's weekly group counselling at the local clinic was encouraging. It made her feel less lonely and knowledgeable about the disease. She learnt how HIV had weakened her immune system, how her T-cells were less than 700 to a thousand, how the higher the number, the stronger would have been her immune system. She was shocked to learn that about half of those living with HIV in Freetown were female.

In the weeks that followed, Virginia became active in the *Médecins sans Frontières* campaign to support women and girls with HIV/AIDS. She joined a group that did house-to-house counselling. In a thundering stream of words, she encouraged people living with HIV and TB to take their drugs regularly, to practice safe sex. She exerted a powerful sway over many, encouraging them to do a cervical smear or Pap test. She told them about a virus in the cervix commonly found in HIV infected females.

* * *

A few months later, Virginia suspected that Samson was cheating on her while she was on her sensitization trips. On the evening she caught Samson leaving his bedroom with a woman, she could hardly believe her eyes. When he returned home from seeing the woman off, Virginia approached him in tears. She had loved him so much that she had made herself susceptible to anxious hysterics filled with suspicion.

"Who is she to you?" she asked him. A sob got choked in her throat.

"She's my cousin," he said, and glanced furtively over his shoulder.

"Don't toy with my affection for you, Samson. Promiscuity doesn't pay . . ."

"Forget it," he said. Her concern sometimes annoyed him.

"How can I forget it?"

"I'm saying the truth."

"No, you're not. Damn liar!"

"Don't you dare talk to me like that," he said furiously.

"I will. You stinking cheat," she said.

Virginia took a step forward. Her right hand shot up and landed mercilessly on Samson's face, sending him staggering back with a suppressed groan. Within the twinkling of an eye, Samson returned the slap. It came down so hard that Virginia fell to the floor. She struggled to get up as a sharp pain tore through her body.

"Never slap me again," he said, reaching out as if to help her. But, instead, he gave her a kick on her buttocks which sent her sprawling on the floor once more. Cursing softly she got to her feet and beat the dust off her faded blouse and skirt.

"Get out of here!" he screamed at her, as he started packing her few belongings into a big colourful *Ghana-must-go* bag.

"Are you treating me this way because of another woman?" she stammered, tears rolling down her eyes.

"No but because you slapped me," he said.

"I slapped you because you're a cheating liar," she said.

"Get out of here, now!" he screamed at her again, and threw her bag of belongings outside.

Virginia bit her nails and cursed herself for being in love with such a scoundrel. She wondered why Samson had recently become so aloof and unreasonable towards her. Was it because of her health status? Or was her beauty becoming a fading illusion? She asked herself.

"I'm leaving but you'll pay for this one day," she said as she grabbed her bag and left.

A wind was stirring from the sea, blowing across the moon-lit fishing hamlet. A small group of busy-body neighbours were already gathered outside gossiping about the commotion between Virginia and Samson. She ignored them and walked away thinking about where she could go. Samson's behaviour seemed to have deepened her plight. The urge to find her relatives revisited her even though they had shunned her since she took to prostitution. Aunty Sally who was a seamstress and the younger sister of her late mother might be the only one who might show sympathy for her. The mere thought of it made her excited. She increased her pace towards Dove Cut where her aunty lived.

Trudging through streets crowded with people, Virginia arrived at the communal compound of Aunty Sally sweating. She had to walk about two miles from Katakoumbay, as she had no money for the bus fare. At first, Aunty Sally could not recognize her niece whom she had not seen in some years. Once she did, she screeched like a cat, and rushed to embrace a speechless Virginia.

"Come in, come in, my daughter. Virginia, I'm glad to see you," said Aunty Sally.

"Good evening, aunty," Virginia responded shyly, avoiding eye contact with her emotional aunt.

"Come, take a seat. Give me your bag. You must be thirsty," said Aunty Sally, gently taking the bag from her.

"Thank you, aunty," Virginia said in a soft, scratchy voice.

She was offered a glass of water by her aunt. They sat down silently side by side while Aunty Sally looked intensely at her niece. It was her striking resemblance to her late sister that was amazing — a medley of love and reminiscence permeated her heart. She held her niece's hand in hers. It was cold; there was no life in it.

"What brought you here tonight, my daughter?" Aunty Sally asked.

"I'm homeless, aunty."

"You aren't. My home is yours."

"Thank you, aunty. Thank you so much."

"But why did you stay in that brothel, my daughter?"

A ray of life came into her. She had to defend herself. She could not be so tight-lipped. But as she looked at her aunt she found that her throat had gone dry. Her heartbeat became rapid and even though she felt defenceless, she managed to say, "I had no other place."

"But you could have stayed with me," Aunty Sally countered her defence.

Virginia thought otherwise. Not when she has been introduced to prostitution by Samson. She told Aunty Sally of her health status, and her aspiration of remaining active in the campaign in support of women and girls living with HIV/AIDS. Although Aunty Sally was astonished, she sat listening silently, her dark eyes dull with sadness. She felt all the negative things she had heard about Virginia's lifestyle receding. Aunty Sally saw no need to cry over spilled milk. Why should she bother someone who appeared to be going through an agony of repentance? Her niece seemed to have learnt the bitter lesson that promiscuity could have dire consequences. Virginia felt relieved after explaining herself to Aunty Sally. From then on she made herself comfortable in the one-bedroom apartment of her aunt.

✖ ✖ ✖

Within a couple of weeks after her arrival at Aunty Sally's, Virginia paid a visit to a female doctor in a nearby clinic. To her surprise, she was informed that she was a few weeks pregnant. As she looked at the doctor, she found that her throat became dry. Her heartbeat seemed to have skipped a beat before resuming a rapid rhythm. Momentarily, she shivered with an urge to urinate.

"Pregnant?" she blurted out. "What can I do, doctor?"

"You tell me if you would like to keep it or not," said the doctor, looking at Virginia with infinite pity in her eyes. The words sat heavy on her mind like a log of wood. She wanted a breath of fresh air. For her, it was like peering into a maelstrom of horror. In the silence that followed, the ceiling fan sounded ghostly as if calling for attention. She pondered for only a brief moment before saying boldly, "I'll keep the pregnancy."

"The baby may not be HIV positive," said the doctor.

"So, what's next doctor?"

"Well, you'll maintain the dosage and make sure that you follow the regimen."

Virginia left the clinic thinking of all that had happened to her since she was diagnosed with HIV: her maltreatment at the government pharmacy, the show-down with Mama Ehga, her campaign in support of women and girls living with HIV/AIDS, her dismissal by Samson, and her reunion with Aunty Sally. It almost felt as though all those things had happened to somebody else many years ago.

Although images of her recent meeting with the doctor were still rattling around in her head, Virginia kept reminding herself that in the midst of adversity, much could be achieved. She started coming to grips with reality by taking her drugs regularly and planning for the birth of the baby. Nine months later, Virginia gave birth to a baby boy who was HIV negative. Her health had improved greatly and she decided to be an apprentice seamstress under Aunty Sally's supervision. In the months that followed, Samson paid Virginia a visit. He had only apologies, promising to help raise the child too.

3

Republic Of Ugosoba

Kekuda could move a crowd with his words — he was that eloquent. Over six feet tall, early-thirties, dark and handsome, the people loved him. He had that Barack Obama aura: Determination, diligence, and patience. His patience was like that of a vulture waiting for its prey. Not to mention ambition, for his large, bloodshot eyes and thin lips portrayed a go-getter. He loved women. His ears twitched like that of an elephant at the voice of a woman. He chewed his tongue frequently when thoughtful. On several occasions, he had chewed his tongue so hard that it bled. When he walked, he dragged his feet as if iron chains were clamped on them. He spoke fast like someone with a mouthful of hot rice. For many people in the Republic of Ugosoba, where politics was not for the pure in heart, his name was synonymous with change. Kekuda's adoration was a measure of their gratitude to his determination to topple the government of Sir Kongo Eel, the incumbent despot.

Kekuda was a final year Honours student at the University of Ugosoba studying Political Science and Social Justice. The University had become as much a part of Kekuda as his faded jeans. He has been earmarked for a scholarship to pursue a Masters programme in a white man's land. By becoming president of the National Union of Students, he however did not only make a name for himself but also numerous enemies.

Among those was Sir Kongo Eel, the land's eccentric and ruthless ruler. It was regarded by many as foolhardy for one to be in conflict with Sir Kongo Eel. Having ruled the country for twenty-two years, he regarded his opponents as disgruntled elements that should be eliminated. Within the past couple of years, he had ordered the execution of a number of them. Some ended up in jail, detained for years without trail. He was known to sneer at so-called revolutionaries, radicals, and agitators.

⚔ ⚔ ⚔

One afternoon in the month of March, the scudding black clouds could not deter the noisy crowd of students of the University of Ugosoba from protesting against the deteriorating standard of living in the land. They marched to the ruler's State House carrying banners reflecting their demands, and they held their books aloft. Secondary and primary school pupils had also joined the crowd singing themselves hoarse with vigour:

"No school, no business!
No school, no business!
Kongo Eel must go!
Kongo Eel must go!
Down with Kongo Eel!
Down with Kongo Eel!

The struggle continues!

Yeah, the struggle continues, oh yeah!"

It was as if all the clocks in the land were frozen on that particular day. Every man, woman, and child held their breath. It was said that even the *jinnis* had never seen such a day in their life. The old people of Ugosoba, paralysed by terror in their small corners, sobbed inaudibly like lost souls. The silence of the vultures, perched on the State House's age-old baobab tree, vibrated horribly as there was something ominous behind the silence. For many, they hoped that it was the day of the windfall when Sir Kongo Eel's authoritarian regime would answer to the atrocities it had committed on the people.

People flocked to the streets as never before. The students were joined by jobless ragamuffins, hooligans, and ex-convicts who perpetrated the burning and looting of public and private properties. The protest was on a grand scale. No sooner than expected, scuffles between the protesters and riot police became a bloodbath. Live bullets were fired into the crowd but they stood their ground. Three protesters were shot dead by the police who fired tear gas into the mayhem. A protest that was supposed to be peaceful reached biblical proportion. In the forefront of the protest, Kekuda and his lieutenants were dragging the Vice-Chancellor, Principal, and Warden of the University to the State House where Sir Kongo Eel was patiently waiting in indomitable spirit. He could hear in his mind's ear the blood-stirring insults from these nincompoops. Moreover, he had received information from his Criminal Investigation Department secret agents that the so-called rebellious students wanted to have an audience with him. Since then, this information hovered around in his head like a talismanic chant. He was more than ready to teach them a lesson.

✖ ✖ ✖

Once they entered the State House, Kekuda, nine of his lieutenants, and the three University officials were quickly ushered into Sir Kongo Eel's large flamboyant office. They were offered seats by half a dozen male assistants, all dressed in dark-coloured three-piece suits. Already seated on his golden throne, His Excellency moved his right hand through his gray-haired head and stroked his gray beard. He then adjusted his prescription glasses and slightingly pulled on the lapels of his glittering gold-coloured suit which was made to measure in a white man's land. His immaculate white shirt carried a blood-red necktie. Red was the land's colour.

Like most of his subjects, he did not know his exact age. Rumour had it that he must have been past seventy-two, maybe seventy-three. He was a tall, beefy, broad-faced, dark complexioned man, and he had a slight stoop. He was the very picture of good health. When speaking he always gesticulated with his long arms seemingly pushing the air around him, and people that may be in his way. When he wanted to make a point, his elbows would fan out like an eagle ready to pounce on its prey. And he frequently pounced on those who were drunk with the foolishness of opposing him. He wore a severe and mournful look except when he was being inaugurated as ruler to serve another five-year term. During such occasions, he would become a brilliant orator. His face would beam with joy, reflecting his hunger for recognition and power.

Led by Kekuda, the students lashed out with a litany of demands, ranging from inadequate resources and facilities at the University to the deteriorating standard of living in the land. His Excellency cleared his throat and thanked the entourage for coming to present their case to him out of their own volition. But it was obvious from his bowed head and gnashing teeth that he had something else up his sleeve. When he raised his head, a sort of smile hovered around the edge of his mouth. And with a clear unemotional voice he told his audience how learning and teaching were noble professions whose practitioners were modest and inspired not by self-glory but selfless service — an ideal for all Ugosobians. At this juncture, the student union representative for Culture murmured, "That's your business, we don't care." Not many in the audience heard the comment because all eyes and ears were riveted on the bigger drama on the throne.

"As Ruler and Commander of the Armed Forces of the Republic of Ugosoba, and by the power vested in me as Chancellor of the University of Ugosoba, I hereby implore you to return to your campus, put on your thinking caps, arrive at a consensus, list down your demands, and submit them to me through the Vice-Chancellor of the University. Some of you here would be aware of the fact that some graduates of the University have joined our political party and they have been appointed to various top positions within the government, the military, and the police, and others still in schools and colleges have joined our party's youth wing thereby preparing to become the land's leaders. This should be the path that you should take rather than mobilizing gangsters to burn and loot properties of innocent citizens."

"As some of you must have heard in the media — although a particular newspaper refused to publish it on its front page, our land will soon break away from its economic impasse as oil and natural gas has been discovered offshore. Of course, this will definitely improve our standard of living and bring prosperity to generations yet unborn. Moreover, in the not too distant future, the main towns in the whole land will be electrified as the long-awaited hydropower project will achieve fruition. The Shade Lamp Electricity Company and also the Comot Mawa Water Company will be totally overhauled with a view to eliminating corrupt officials that have been putting our people in unnecessary hardship. Shortly, in terms of food production, a team of experts will be commencing feasibility studies on the use of genetically modified rice grains in the swampy regions of the land. In the same vein, a national committee has recently been set up to find ways to improve the education system, especially in terms of providing more bursaries and scholarships to you people."

Sir Kongo Eel paused to allow the mention of improved educational system to sink in to the minds of his audience. Impulsively, the three University officials started an applause that ended abruptly as nobody else joined them. The threesome felt embarrassed while the ruler struggled to contain his anger.

He stood up to his full height and said to the audience, "Gentlemen, I'll be back in five minutes." He then went into an adjoining room, followed by one of his assistants at whom he glared.

"What do these students think of themselves?" he asked him.

"Ungrateful," replied the assistant, "I was expecting a thunderous applause crowned by a standing ovation," he added.

"I've to be very careful in dealing with these nitwits as they are capable of bringing my downfall."

"You're right, sir."

"Especially since that particular newspaper mentioned that I'm amassing wealth in a foreign bank, and investing in real estate overseas."

"Sir, don't rest on your oars and allow such closely-guarded secrets to be leaked."

"Are you implying that it's true?" Sir Kongo Eel fumed at the assistant.

"No sir, your Excellency, I'm sorry sir."

"I'll not vent my anger on you but after the meeting, I'll like you to call me the Minister of Information."

"Yes, sir, I'll do so."

"Ask him to confirm information about a newspaper article that mentioned my insatiable predilection for uninitiated teenage virgins."

"Yes, sir, I'll do so."

⚜ ⚜ ⚜

Sir Kongo Eel rejoined his audience. As far as he was concerned the moment had come for him to desist from sugar-coating his words. He then continued his address on the seemingly contemptuous audience as if nothing untoward had happened.

"Let it be known to every law-abiding citizen that a few weeks ago, before this illegal protest, I was even planning to release a bunch of political prisoners. I must warn you that though we have encouraged enlightenment, yet the pen could never be mightier than the sword in this Republic."

The students turned to look at each other, seemingly alarmed at Sir Kongo Eel's last statement. A gold-plated clock on the wall solemnly chimed the hour. The University's warden, a retired soldier, stifled a cough. His Excellency continued speaking.

"So your knowledge should be diverted to more productive exploits rather than slander, libel and malicious rumour-mongering. I would hate to see any of you fine gentlemen join the self-styled rebel group, Revolutionary Justice Army, the so-called R.J.A., in the quest to oust me from my God-given office. What some of you malcontents fail to realize is that with all my power, wisdom and profound understanding I could not, like anybody else, argue against the hand of fate. So, you should know by now that my position has been decreed by the Almighty God and as such I will sit on this throne until I die."

With a quick glance at his gold wrist watch, he pushed to conclude his speech by moving his right hand through his head and stroking his beard. He further re-adjusted his glasses and with exaggerated gesticulation of his arms, he continued.

"I would like you to realize that as students, you have always been supported by the tax-payers money. Most of you have been provided with bursaries to further your education, fed three times a day, and are practically living in an ivory tower. So, don't be carried away by illusions and become like the river that forgot its source and ran dry. I've heard your demands and you've heard the government's point of view, so I will not waste any more of your time or mine. As you may be aware my office has always been as busy as an anthill. Therefore, as I mentioned earlier, I would like you to return to your campus, list down your demands and submit them to me through the appropriate authorities. Thereafter, we'll act accordingly and see how we can work together and unfurl certain plans that have been in the pipeline. Remember, though, that the goat that escaped slaughter on Christmas Day will not escape the knife on New Year's Day. A word for the wise should be sufficient. You may take your leave. Thank you."

⌘ ⌘ ⌘

As it turned out, the demands of the students were still not met six months later. The dining halls on the University campus were shut down as students were now expected to purchase their own food instead of being fed by the government. Bursaries and scholarships were hard to come by as students struggled to pay their fees, and buy their books. The student union bus service to and from the University, like the electricity and water supplies, became unreliable.

Ugosoba as a nation was going through the throes of electricity and water supply crises. Hardship forced some students to become prostitutes, pimps, and gamblers. Others traded in cigarettes, alcohol, marijuana, and psychedelic drugs. The University authorities placed an indefinite ban on all radical fraternity and sorority groups and newsletters. Ironically, while some lecturers were resigning their positions in droves in search of greener pastures, others were having a field day deeply involved in sexual relationships with their students. Life on the University campus was now unbearable for many.

In these low moments, the student union, led by Kekuda, thought that it was time for another protest against the government. However, not every student was ready for another confrontation with the brute force of the riot police. One night, while Kekuda and his lieutenants were trying to mobilize students for another protest, he was confronted by a female student, a Tarzan of a lady.

"Mister Freedom Fighter, why would you fool people to tread where angels fear to tread?" she cried hysterically.

It was said so seriously and so bluntly that Kekuda was speechless. He had not expected a challenge from a female student. He knew that most female students were uninterested in campus politics. Although he felt perplexed, at last he responded rather sharply, "Madam, I don't fool anybody, besides we're all adults who know their left from their right."

"But you know quite well that we can't fight the government by hitting the streets. After six months of waiting, what have they done for us? Not a mere glimpse of light. It's a waste of time," she said.

"I don't think so. The beginning is always difficult but if we persevere, things are bound to improve. We can't remain complacent about the scheme of things," said Kekuda.

"Mister, after all that we've done our lives have not changed in any way," she added. "You should know by now that you can't be armed with expectations from a government of semi-literates and thugs."

Kekuda was silent for a while, and then began very slowly as he groped for words: "But if we don't show our discontent, would the authorities know our predicament?"

"They don't care and they'll never care. So stop canvassing for students to join a doomed protest in which they'll be injured or shot at by the police."

"Our last protest was a general consensus among students, and I never incited anybody," said Kekuda, showing signs of irritation.

"Well, I would like to complete my studies and leave this place as soon as possible instead of being deterred by protests. I've enough deterrence to contend with already, so don't add salt to injury," said the Tarzan of a lady.

He saw there was no hope along the present line of argument. He even knew all along that an uncle of this particular female student was the Permanent Secretary at the Ministry of Information and Broadcasting.

"Don't be selfish, madam. The aspiration of students is to complete their studies, so you're not alone. We need to unite in order to achieve our common goals — freedom and justice. So we . . . ," Kekuda was interrupted by the student.

"Have you heard the rumour that the government is now determined to arrest the ring-leaders of any future protest and even expel them from the University?" she asked slowly and walked away.

Although Kekuda had not heard this rumour, he was not surprised, as he was partly prepared to face the worst. What made him feel plunged into a depth of frustration was to have heard it from someone whom he suspected to be a government spy. *But then why had she referred to officials in the government as semi-literates and thugs? Well, weren't spies known to be like double-edged knives?* He asked himself.

✵ ✵ ✵

As Kekuda walked to his residence on campus that night he turned over in his mind the female student's remark about the impending and threatened arrest and expulsion of ring-leaders. He thought of going to his room but decided on second thought to see if there were students at the outdoor student gathering area called Addis. It was there he was informed by a male student that a group of policemen were out to arrest him and some other students. He decided to leave the campus immediately.

The memories of his mother flooded his mind. *Was this one of the dire consequences his mother warned him about?* He wondered. Aided by the darkness of night, he took a bush footpath that would lead him to the home of Saidu, his cousin, where he planned to hide out until he was able to leave the country and its menace. He knew that he was in for a long haul.

⚵ ⚵ ⚵

Later that night while in hiding in Saidu's shack, Kekuda peeped through a window. The sky over Gutter-Yais, one of the numerous seaside slums in Ugosoba, was overcast with heavy black clouds and a strong wind was blowing sand, litter and dry leaves. Suddenly, there was a thunderbolt that scared him out of his wits. It reminded him of the superstition that a thunderbolt would crash on those who stole the chickens of others. Soon it began to rain, first a pitter-patter, and then it came down in large, sharp drops like those of the monsoon.

He listened to the sound of the rain falling on the corrugated iron sheet roof and the dogs wailing restlessly in the bad weather. Shivering, he recalled with fond memories the warnings of his mother, Amina. She never wanted Kekuda to be involved in politics. On several occasions, after consulting her oracle, she has warned him of the dire consequences that awaited him as a politician. She applied various ways of dissuasion but Kekuda's heart was hardened and Amina finally gave him up as lost. Unlike Amina, who had literally been swept away by the torrents of events in Ugosoba, Kekuda was ready to fight in a land that had become the Mecca of bigotry and prejudice.

In the morning of his first day in hiding, Kekuda heard the news over the radio that all so-called radical groups at the University have been banned; himself and most of his colleagues had been expelled from the University and that the police were searching every nook and cranny looking for him. He felt cornered like a rat being chased by a cat. His appetite for food was lost for the better part of the day.

Maybe if he smoked a roll of marijuana he would gain some appetite, and even if he did not regain his appetite, he would at least forget the turn his life had taken. Kekuda never did drugs. Now he asked his cousin to fetch him some marijuana. He lit up, closed his eyes and inhaled some of its smoke. He coughed as the smoke burned his lungs and throat. As he felt his head pounding, he decided that smoking marijuana was not the solution to his problems.

In the dead of night, thanks to Saidu's meagre cash savings, Kekuda was spirited away like a condemned prisoner by some fishermen. As the saying goes, there are better things in life than money but it just takes money to get them. Maybe better things might be waiting for him as he headed out of his land into the neighbouring land Totonou in a dug-out canoe with an outboard engine.

Although the sea was calm for most of the two-day journey, he experienced seasickness on the first night. In order to stop his vomiting, one of the fishermen asked him to drink a bowlful of sea water and this stopped the vomiting. For food, they shared with him their biscuits, bread and sardines. Once he was ashore, he asked for directions to the campus of the University of Totonou where he would meet one Joe Blay, a student union leader with whom he had been in contact over the years.

✘ ✘ ✘

The sun had set a couple of hours before, and a cool night breeze was blowing gently. Twinkling stars could be seen dancing in the clear sky as if celebrating the appearance of the moon. Kekuda was reminded of Ugosoba, and was filled with nostalgia for a country in which he was now a fugitive.

Walking beside him was Joe Blay. He was looking simple but soldierly in his military fatigue. He was the type of man who could persevere doggedly on the cobbled floor. They entered the University's botanical garden and sat down on a bench to discuss Kekuda's intention to join the Revolutionary Justice Army.

"I chose for us to meet in this garden at night because, you'll soon learn, most of our meetings are held in the bush under the cover of darkness," Joe Blay stated in a cold tone.

"So how do I go about meeting the leader?" Kekuda inquired impatiently.

"I'll give you a sealed and confidential letter which you'll deliver personally to Captain Cobra, our leader."

"Where do I meet him?"

"She is a woman," Joe Blay corrected Kekuda. "You'll travel by bus and get off at a town called Gba, and then you'll contact one Sissy Juliet whose address is written on this paper," Joe Blay continued, handing over a neatly written address.

"And then?" asked Kekuda.

"Sissy Juliet will then take you to Captain Cobra," said Joe Blay.

This whole episode reminded Kekuda of the wisdom in the saying that before people embark on a journey of revenge they should dig two graves. He wondered if he was ready to dig those graves, he only knew that he was ready for the journey.

"I need some money and clothes for this trip," Kekuda whispered instinctively as if afraid for the cool night breeze to blow his words away.

"I'll see to that," Joe Blay nodded in agreement, and asked if there was any other question. As there was none, their secret meeting ended as abruptly as it started.

⚸ ⚸ ⚸

It was now three days after his meeting with Joe Blay. Early that morning as the sun was rising, Kekuda tried to suppress the nausea he felt from the smell of gun powder. A mixture of fear, frustration, and curiosity rooted him in the line-up of fighters. He had always been terrified of guns; the mention of it made his body quiver. But now as part of the muster parade standing at attention in front of Captain Cobra, he had made up his mind to be trained as a rebel.

At six feet tall, fair in complexion with a striking beauty that could steal a man's heart, Captain Cobra was a no-nonsense woman. She was the head of the bush training camp far away from the watchful eyes of the capital city. Always in military fatigue, she had been with the Revolutionary Justice Army for five years, and fought several battles against the government forces. She had been arrested twice by government forces but cunningly escaped from their grip. In the training camp, she was also known as Mammy Water, a name given to a beautiful female *jinni*.

After the muster parade, a dark complexioned muscular rebel who introduced himself as Rambo, took Kekuda aside and asked him:

"When did you join this group? I haven't seen you before."

Kekuda assessed Rambo who stood six-three, wearing military fatigue that covered a thick, ebony body. He had a crazy look in his eyes. His wild dreadlocks made him truly appear insane.

"I was recruited recently. I came from Ugosoba where I was a university student union leader. I've now been expelled for organizing an anti-government protest."

"Oh, I see, you're the wanted man. The famous Kekuda whose name is on your national radio," he said, smiling.

"Yes, I'm the one," Kekuda giggled, proudly.

"I'm also from Ugosoba," said Rambo, reaching out for a handshake.

"Wow! So we're brothers," said Kekuda.

"Yes. Comrades, you mean, planning a revenge on Sir Kongo Eel," said Rambo, winking his left eye at Kekuda.

"Yes, I plan to lead an invasion into the country, destabilize all walks of life, and bring down the government," said Kekuda.

Rambo laughed like a hyena at the words of Kekuda, and abruptly chuckled. "That makes the two of us." He drew closer to Kekuda and whispered in his ear: "do you know the implications of what you've just said? It's treason; a crime punishable by death."

Kekuda swallowed hard. "I do."

"I'm a rebel, remember. You don't know me from Adam," Rambo said, breathing warm breath on him.

In a couple of weeks, Kekuda completed his training in guerrilla warfare under the tutelage of Captain Cobra and Rambo. On several occasions, the three of them led groups of armed insurgents across the border into the neighbouring Republic of Ugosoba and attacked military, police, and civilian facilities. Those who survived the cross-fire were hacked to death or their limps, ears, lips and noses mutilated.

Within this time Kekuda studied revolutionary teachings by leaders like Sekou Touré, Kwame Nkrumah, Modibo Keita, Walter Rodney, and read books written by Frantz Omar Fanon. Captain Cobra, on the advice of the ruling council of the Revolutionary Justice Army, willing abdicated her leadership responsibilities to Kekuda. The group needed not only a zealous revolutionary but also some-body with a good education like Kekuda. Rambo became his body guard. The fight against the regime of Sir Kongo Eel lasted for more than half a decade before a truce was reached. Under the leadership of Kekuda, the Revolutionary Justice Army was asked to disarm and join the government of Sir Kongo Eel.

✵ ✵ ✵

It was mid-morning, and Kekuda and his entourage was on their way to Totonou airport so that they could travel to Ugosoba in order to form a new government. It was raining heavily and it looked like a bigger storm would follow. On arrival at the airport, just as the bigger storm became violent, he learnt that the flight was delayed indefin-itely, until the storm passed. He was alarmed by the news, feeling strangely shaken. His tongue moved dryly on his lips, his eyes red-dened as if waiting to be gouged out.

The air conditioning system in the airport was dead. The heat was excruciating. The fabric of the gown that he was wearing became uncomfortably itchy around his neck. He looked at the airport staff with a stern uncompromising expression. He had been blinded by power and forgot that a storm could stop him from reaching his goal.

It seemed as if his head-on charge to rule the Republic of Ugosoba was becoming elusive, after all his years in rebellion. There was nothing he could do now but wait for the storm to pass.

Kekuda was rudely stirred from his thoughts when a group of Totonou soldiers and policemen approached him and his entourage. They were surprised to see so many armed men encircling them. One of the soldiers, whose rank indicated that he was a Major, walked up to Kekuda and said, "Sir, you're under arrest."

Kekuda stared at the soldier, his mind spinning, his need for the Vice-Presidency expanding like a dark and threatening thundercloud filling up his mind. His wildly dilated eyes told the story of the hunger in him, the fire that could never be snuffed, born out of the thirst for power.

The Major's next words sounded very far away when Kekuda heard them, "Move!" "Move!"

For weeks afterward, he'd wake up in the small hours of the night washed in sweat, with the word "*move!*" still falling off his lips.

Once the storm passed, Kekuda and his entourage were flown to Ugosoba where they were placed in custody and indicted by a Special Court. The court served as a forum for reconciliation where victims and perpetrators of human rights violations during the conflict narrated their stories.

On the first day of his trial, Kekuda stood inside the witness box, dumb-founded, not knowing what to say or do until he was handcuffed and dragged into a Black Maria. He felt like weeping but no tears came. Why was life so unjust to him? He wondered. The case against him continued having the same surreal quality to it. It never came to an end as Kekuda died while in incarceration. In less than a year, Sir Kongo Eel was overthrown and murdered in a military coup d'état.

4

A Jamaican In Canada

I dashed up the road like a ballistic missile, the soles of my shoes beating on the pavement, and pushed through the narrow doors into the public telephone booth. I grabbed the receiver, inserted some coins, and dialled a number.

A hoarse female voice responded to the call: "Hello!"

"Is this Esther?" I asked.

"Yes, it is", the voice replied.

"You don't sound well, mom," I said in my deep oratory voice that resonated through the panels of the telephone booth.

"I'm dying, Kwame. Dying from breast cancer," replied mom.

"What?" I asked, shivering from the windy Canadian spring morning.

"My doctor here in Jamaica just broke the news," she said, drawing a deep breath.

I felt a lurch in my chest. "You mean . . . ," I was cut short by mom sobbing and breathing heavily.

"I may die within three months."

"Die?" I asked, searching for words to express myself while adjusting my sunglasses.

"I need five hundred dollars to start the chemotherapy," she said.

I listened with silent concern, robbed of my eloquence for which mom knew me.

"I'm sorry to hear about this mom, but I'm still job-searching," I said, rubbing my bearded jaw.

"Don't worry. Of late, I know that your love for me is unconditional," she said.

"I'm sure that I'll find a job pretty soon," I assured her with my usual positive conviction and stubborn perseverance when facing a challenge.

"Be careful though and don't go to extremes." She had never said so to me since I left the Island. Fear gripped my guts.

"I won't, and once I get a job, I'll send you some money," I promised.

"Just continue to be well-mannered. By the way, Happy Birthday," she said coughing weakly.

"Thank you. But at twenty-three, I feel like a teenager."

"Keep it up, and please give me a call again tomorrow."

"I will," I said and hung up.

Outside the public telephone booth, dark clouds loomed over the city like the sword of Damocles. I pulled my jacket's hood over my head which carried jet-black dreadlocks. Lean, dark in complexion, I looked shorter than my six-foot frame – no thanks to the perpetual stoop to my shoulders. My brown eyes peered out from under trimmed black brows, drilling, as my closest friend often told me, into whatever or whoever I looked at.

A chilly wind blew south into downtown Woodstock, and beat at me. Gusts plastered my coat to my back, whipped the baggy jeans around my legs. I wished my coat was thicker, or that I had worn an extra sweater. As I struggled against the wind, the black Nike sports bag that was dangling from my shoulder became a burden. So, I drifted absentmindedly towards the Dundas Street Tim Hortons café where I had an appointment with my friend, Faya Bourne.

"Hello Kwame. Quite windy outside," Faya greeted me with a smile as he fidgeted his left earring.

I nodded in agreement, and added, "My mother is dying."

Faya gazed at me with quizzical bloodshot eyes. "You mean the old lady is not well?" he muttered taking off a green, red, black and gold-coloured toque from the dreadlocks on his head.

"Yes, recently diagnosed with breast cancer," I replied.

"*Jah* forbid!" he cried, pulling at his beard that had gone partly grey. He was just thirty-five.

"I wish her well," he added.

"I know. But why would she fall ill at this time when I'm still unemployed?"

"Be courageous, my friend. I know you for being good at accepting the unexpected," said Faya.

I smiled and nodded.

"And your father, Roger, died just last year," he continued.

I kept quiet, memories of my dad rushing through my mind.

"What was he like?" Faya asked. "I mean your father, Roger."

I lifted my face to an overhead lamp. "Close your eyes," I said.

"What?"

"Close your eyes," I repeated.

Faya hesitated, then did as I said, wondering what it was all about.

"Feel that warmth on your face?" I asked.

"Yes, I do," he replied.

"Can you see, hear and smell?" I asked him.

"I can see light behind my eyelids, hear sounds, and smell coffee," he continued.

"That's what dad did for me," I said. "He made me feel keen."

"You must have missed him," he said sadly.

"Indeed," I agreed.

"Well, let's see if we can get a job at the tobacco plantation," he said with hopeful eyes.

"Let's go then," I said, as we left the café into the windy afternoon.

As usual, Faya wore a blue jean jacket and blue pants on top of whatever he had underneath his six feet stature. Like me, his practice of the Rastafarian culture, his dark complexion, made him stand out wherever he went. I came to know Faya about a month ago. He seemed to be a calm and easy-going man. If nothing else, our friendship was perhaps based on the feelings that both of us were from Jamaica, and we were no more comfortable in our host country than its people were with us.

Although unable to complete secondary school education, I was proud to be called Kwame, meaning in Akan, a son born on a Saturday. I had neither brothers nor sisters in the John family whose ancestors originated from Ghana. At times I wished I had siblings to fight with, to make life a little more interesting. After my father died from a chronic heart disease, I was as restless as a He-Goat.

So, one day, I attempted to stow myself away on a fishing boat leaving Jamaica for Africa. The aim was to retrace my ancestral roots that were uprooted by the infamous slave traders that I will never, ever forgive. However, before the boat left the port, I was caught by the crew who asked me to take twelve lashes on my bare rump or be handed over to the police. I opted for the lashes, which were so painstakingly meted out, that I was unable to sit down for several days. My buttocks were so sore that they seemed to belong to another body.

Many months after this episode, I became relatively content with life, easy as a pie. Almost daily, I would sit on the coconut-dotted beach in Montego Bay, listening to reggae music, and watching the sun go down the horizon, awestruck by its brilliance. Any form of change would have been resisted by my youthful mind. Unlike most youths in my community, neither alcohol nor tobacco or cannabis won my interest.

I was not so sure whether working as a migrant in Canada was worth the challenge and expense of dodging immigration officials, and living in hardship. At times, I felt my courage waning like a departing moon, in a society that increasingly made no sense to me. I felt alienated and unwelcomed in a place where greetings were uncommon, and smiles were artificial; a place where almost everybody walked with hands in their pockets. I did not want my mother to know about the hardship I was undergoing, not when she was suffering from cancer. That would have been adding salt to injury. So, I decided to face the challenge.

✖ ✖ ✖

While going to the tobacco plantation, we walked in silence and as fast as we could. Dark clouds continued to loom as if it was going to rain. We must reach our destination before the weather becomes worse, I thought. When I saw the plantation I knew it was the place to be employed. Rows and rows of tobacco plants spread out like the tentacles of an octopus. Farm machinery abounded here and there against the background of a Victorian-style mansion dazzling in the daylight. Luxuriant low hedges surrounded the plantation. We were amazed at the prosperous-looking environment. No doubt, there was money to be made here, I thought. As restless as ants, Faya and I joined the sprawling queue of labourers, waiting anxiously for jobs. We were the only Blacks. The rest were all Caucasian men.

Faya was eighth in the queue while three others and I stood behind him. A skinny-looking man next to me was saying, "The farm owner was pretty generous last year."

"He was generous in what way?" I asked him.

"Oh, he paid us two dollars above the minimum wage," he said, licking his lips.

"That was nice of him," I said.

"Well, since he lost his wife and two children in a winter road accident, he had been trying to bend backwards to be fair to all," he added.

"Let's see how it goes this year," I said, turning away from him, as a way to discontinue further conversation. For me, there was only one thing to do; wait patiently like a vulture. The chilly wind enveloped us with pestilential resolve.

The gates of the plantation swung open. A stern-faced red-haired young man shouted, "First seven in the queue, come in!" It took us a moment to understand the man. And then, we became stunned and frustrated by the realization that we were not among the lucky seven.

"Damn it," cried Faya.

"Never despair, my friend," I encouraged him.

"But this is unbelievable," he stammered.

"I'll get a job at all cost. Mom needs my support," I added as if assuring myself.

"When am I going to be as confident as you, Kwame?" he asked.

"The time you see life as a challenge to be conquered, I answered.

"I don't know what to do next," he said.

"Let's go to the job recruitment agency downtown," I pointed out, leading the way.

The dark clouds have cleared and it did not seem as if it was going to rain anymore.

⌘ ⌘ ⌘

When we arrived at the recruitment agency, the sound of a telephone ringing on the receptionist's desk broke the graveyard-like silence in the office. The receptionist, a petite brunette with blue eyes, faded pink lips on her pale face, asked us to sit down before answering the telephone. I sat down beside Faya with the conviction that I'll be offered a job. Faya straddled his seat like someone feeling a nervous clutch in his belly. He looked bereft, arms folded on his chest. He must have envied my confident calm. I needed to be relaxed, if for nothing else but to get a job and help my mother. Once again, I became excited at the possibility of being employed.

"Hi. How can I help you?" the receptionist asked us after her telephone conversation.

"We're seeking employment," I responded.

"What kind of job?" she asked.

"Farm or factory job will do." I said.

She reached out for a bunch of papers and gave them to us.

"Please complete these job application forms," she said.

It took us about thirty minutes to complete the forms. While reviewing them, she called out: "Why didn't you write your social insurance number?"

I hesitated briefly and replied, "We don't have one."

"Then you're ineligible for work," she said.

I became timid and humble. My eyes could not meet hers.

"I'll accept a job that doesn't require the number," I said.

"No, you shouldn't be here," she said dismissively, pushing her hair back.

I tasted bitterness in my mouth. Inside me, something shrank.

"Madam, have you ever been a stranger in a foreign land?" I asked her.

"What do you mean?" she replied with a quizzical glance.

I forced tears to swarm up in my eyes but I did not let them out.

"Look at my eyes," I said.

"Why?

"My mom is dying and I need a job to support her," I said looking almost defiantly.

"Sir, I'm sorry but I can't help you."

I doubted if this petite brunette knew what hardship meant. I shrugged with a sense of defeat. I did not even notice Faya gesturing to me to leave, until he nudged me. I turned slowly and walked towards the exit, trailing him.

✄ ✄ ✄

Once outside the office, we were approached by a slim, medium-height Caucasian man, presumably in his twenties. He wore brown jeans and a black Tee-shirt. He was standing by the main entrance of the office building; and as if he has been eavesdropping on our conversation with the brunette, he beamed at us.

"Hi guys were you able to get a job?" he asked.

As we did not reply to his question, he added

"I wonder why. This agency is currently offering jobs to people," he said, puffing smoke from a cigarette.

"No social insurance number," I said.

"I can help you to get one," he proposed, scratching his bald head atop a face that carried sunken blue eyes.

Another agent of false hope, I thought, glancing at him suspiciously as he threw out a skull-and-bones-tattooed hand for a shake.

"How can you do that?" asked Faya, shaking his hands. I did not.

"I can borrow you a social insurance number for a fee," he murmured, fidgeting with his heavy silver necklace.

"How much would it cost?" I asked as memories of my ailing mother rattled around my head.

"It'll cost you ten percent of your wages," he replied with a sly smile.

"I'll go for it", I said desperately, deciding to trust him.

"For a start, I need fifty dollars," he said.

I counted the money from my wallet and gave it to him. He reached inside his pocket and fished out a social insurance card, which he gave to me.

"Call me Dwight. You provide me with your name, address, and a telephone number," he said.

"It's a deal," I said.

✖ ✖ ✖

Four weeks later, after an appointment with Dwight, I was still unemployed. We scheduled another meeting between him, Faya and me in one of the cafés downtown. He was late. He joined us at a table after ordering a cup of coffee and a banana muffin.

"Any luck in finding a job?" he asked me without greeting us or apologizing for being late. I shook my head in response.

"I can't believe you," he burst out in anger. "Someone saw you working in a chicken farm."

"That wasn't me," I said.

"Let's go outside, too many folks listening", he said, staggering out of the café as we followed him.

"Listen, I hardly do business with idiots like you." He paused as if waiting for our response, which he did get.

"Damn you! Who do you think you are?" Faya cried, shaking with anger.

"A cocaine sniffer looking for a jail term," Dwight replied, wiping his runny nose with the back of his right hand.

"Who cares? You should be looking for a death term," I said.

"I swear, by my damn stripper of a mother, you'll pay for this," Dwight sneered, walking away from us.

I looked briefly in Faya's direction, but his eyes were darting uncontrollably as if he wanted to fight but wanted to be sure that we were alone.

"Faya, let's leave this place," I said.

A couple of years ago, there were a lot of things I could have done to a guy like Dwight. Least of all, I could have reacted rudely if not violently to him. Those were the days when I was neither interested in finding a job nor cared about anybody, not even my parents. By then, I was spontaneous in all I do. I hardly spoke up, and always ready to give up easily when the going got tough. In a nutshell, I lacked ambition.

Now though, with Dwight gone his way, we melted into the bustling downtown in frustration. Sunset crawled in before we decided to head home.

✖ ✖ ✖

Just then, we were confronted by a police officer on foot patrol.

"Can I see your photo IDs?" the tall beefy-looking man growled.

Solemnly, we handed over our entry permit cards. He peered at them with haughty, hazel-coloured eyes that oddly seemed out of sync with his missing left ear lobe.

"Expired entry permit cards," he said to Faya, as if he was responsible for both of us. He put the offending ID in his pocket – together with mine.

"Now search your pockets and bring out everything," he said, smiling slyly.

We dipped our hands into our pockets and came up with one hundred and twenty dollars in total which we handed to him.

"What's in that sports bag dangling from your shoulder?" the officer barked at me, scratching his bald head.

"Personal belongings," I replied with confidence.

"You must have stolen them, right?"

"No, they're mine."

"And where do you live?"

"I live . . ."

"I mean both of you," he snapped, wagging his finger at us.

"We live together," jumped in Faya.

"I asked where!" thundered the officer.

"We live here in Woodstock," said Faya.

"Oh, I see, you're the trouble-makers in town."

"No, we're not" I replied.

"Where are you from?"

"We're from Jamaica," I replied with renewed confidence, just to allay his suspicion.

"Why can't you people stay in your country?" he asked.

We reserved our comments.

"What's your name?"

"I'm Kwame John."

"And you?"

"Faya Bourne."

"What?" he asked frowning.

"Faya Bourne," my friend snarled at him.

The officer laughed.

"You shall report at the police station by 8 a.m. tomorrow. Now, run before I count three," said the officer.

We were speechless but shrugged off our bewilderment. We ran away like Olympic sprinters until we came to a stop in a dark alley where I made out the silhouette of a man standing with his back towards us. We realized that it was Dwight urinating drunkenly against a brick wall with not a care in the world.

Faya glanced at me and decided to grab at what he thought was an opportunity. Silently, Faya tiptoed behind Dwight. His hands closed around a club he picked up. As Dwight turned around, Faya raised his arms and, with great force, swung the club. The weapon landed on his nape. An uncontrollable sound of panic froze in Dwight's throat as he dropped down unconscious. I looked at Faya, alarmed. Even in the poor light, I could see that his eyes had suddenly become bloodshot, as red as fire.

Panic-stricken, we took to our heels in opposite directions. While I headed home against my better judgement, Faya did not. After running for about five minutes, I stopped, turned around to see if I was being followed. My heartbeat slowing, I murmured to myself, "That was interesting."

The one-bedroom apartment that I shared with Faya was on the outskirts of town, among a shapeless conglomerate of dilapidated farm barns. The smell of cow dung was a constant. I hardly slept right through the night.

⚒ ⚒ ⚒

The next day, when two policemen came to arrest me, the door was open and hot air hung at the entrance. I was charged with first-degree murder, throwing me off balance. I would never, ever think of murdering someone. I was surprised and felt betrayed by Faya's failure to take responsibility for his act. I wondered though if I should blame him for not coming home. Maybe, I was a fool to have come home. Meanwhile, I felt resentment for the police that I would give anything to overcome.

While in custody and during interrogation, I learnt from the police that a search was on for Faya. All seemed lost, and my goal of finding a job appeared to be unachievable.

I could not afford the services of a lawyer to defend the charge against me. I wondered what I was going to do. Could I defend myself? I worried. My court date was the next day. My thoughts were interrupted by a police officer rapping his baton against the bars of my cell.

"You have a visitor," he announced.

I held out my hands to him to be handcuffed. I was presumed a dangerous person. When he had secured my hands, he opened my cell and led me out to the common area. I was wondering who knew me enough in a foreign land to bother about me, when he indicated a table where a Caucasian man was already seated.

"Meet your lawyer," the police officer said and walked away. Slowly, I sat down on the vacant chair across from my guest. He was a short, heavy-set and strong man that looked to be in his forties.

"My name is Clinton Greene," he said.

"Kwame John," I said. "I don't have any money, sir. I can't pay you," I told him.

He laughed. "Do not worry, Mr. John. I am paid by the government," he said.

"The same government that pays the lawyer that would prosecute me?" I asked.

"Yes. I can see where you are heading, Mr. John," said Greene. "However, you must relax. This is not a case of a piper's paymaster dictating the tune. I am on your side. I am from the Public Defender's office."

"Okay," I said, not exactly understanding what he was saying, but not keen to make a fool of myself either. I resolved to clear my name no matter what it took. However, I knew my life would never be the same again whatever the outcome. Suddenly, I wondered if my lawyer was any good.

"How many cases have you won?" I blurted out without thinking, afraid that I would stop myself if I gave the issue some thought.

"It is not that simple," said Greene. "Winning or losing a case is not the most important thing in a case for a lawyer."

"How many cases?" I repeated, with some impatience.

"None," answered Greene.

Oh great! Just the lawyer I need, I thought with a sinking feeling. And with mounting apprehension, I wondered if I would be found guilty or not.

✖ ✖ ✖

By mid-morning, the Woodstock courtroom looked like a sea of heads. Hushed, muffled whispers rippled through the audience. My eyes darted from one corner of the room to the next as I started singing softly Bob Marley's *Crazy Baldheads*:

Build your penitentiary; we build your schools,
Brainwash education to make us the fools.
Hate is your reward for our love,
Telling us of your God above.

"Keep quiet," the guard next to me murmured.

I kept quiet and thought, "I got to survive this one".

I stood in the accused box looking at a possible stiff sentence.

"Get a grip," I checked myself silently, "can't be scared. Not yet."

I shifted from one foot to the other. The few days in jail made me feel older than my age. In dirty clothes, with my head down, hands in handcuffs, I thought about my sick mother in Montego Bay. Those thoughts were interrupted by the authoritative masculine voice of the judge's clerk.

"All rise. Crown Court for the Province of Ontario, Woodstock Branch, is now in session, the Honourable Deborah Macmillan presiding," he announced.

Macmillan entered the courtroom in black robes and white wig. She appeared to be in her early sixties, just below six feet and slender. She went for her high-backed chair and sat down. "You may be seated," she said to the audience.

The silence was briefly broken as people took their seats. She gazed out at her courtroom through her glasses that sat on her face like a permanent fixture.

"To start with, the public is here as observers, and not participants," she said. "I'll not tolerate nonsense from anybody. If you do nonsense, you go to jail. Do I make myself clear?"

There was arctic silence.

"The clerk will call the case," said the judge.

"Docket number 5c/SCWO/2003, Queen Regina versus Kwame John," intoned the clerk, reading it off the top of a folder.

"Appearances," the judge called.

The prosecutor stood up. In his late fifties, short and fat with a baby-like face, Rogers was known as a daredevil in Woodstock legal circles. "Your honour, my name is Dave Rogers. I appear with J. H. Swift for the Crown."

My lawyer stood up. "May it please the court," he began. "My name is Clinton Greene. I appear for Kwame John, the accused."

And then the clerk read the charges, which contained one count of conspiracy to murder and one count of murder.

"How do you plead? Guilty or not guilty?" the clerk asked me.

"Not guilty," I said, wondering if anybody had heard the quaver in my voice.

My lawyer then applied for my bail – which the prosecutor opposed. But after hearing arguments from both sides, the judge made her decision.

"The defendant is admitted to bail," said the judge. "Bail is set at one hundred thousand dollars. Trial starts in two weeks. That is," she said, consulting her diary, "July the seventh. Adjourned!"

✵ ✵ ✵

During the two weeks interval, a number of Canadian citizens were selected at random and summoned for jury duty. And in the last three days before trial, the jury was selected and empanelled: seven males and five females. Eight of them were white while the rest were blacks. There were three alternate jurors– all white. The selection process had been long and exhausting, with my lawyer using all of his peremptory strikes. But he seemed happy with the outcome.

"The possibility of your getting a fair trial is now much higher," he told me.

And then the trial day was finally upon us.

"All rise!" the clerk called out as Justice Macmillan made her entrance.

"You may be seated," said the judge after taking her seat. "Bring in the jury."

Seven males and five females filed into the court and into the jury box.

"Good morning all!" Macmillan greeted. She glanced at Dave Rogers, the prosecutor. "Is the prosecution ready to proceed?"

"We're ready, Your Honour," said Rogers.

"Very well then," said Macmillan. "Clerk, call the case."

The case was called and appearances announced. The prosecutor turned to the jury and began his opening statement.

"Ladies and gentlemen, the Crown will present to you irrefutable evidence of the offence of murder." The prosecutor cleared his throat, adjusted his robe and then his wig. "After you've seen the evidence and heard the witnesses, you will be required to deliver a verdict as to whether on June 3, 2003 Kwame John did not maliciously murder Dwight Longman. The province will show that the motive for this crime is hate. We will call witnesses who will testify that the defendant made insulting remarks to the victim out of pure hatred." Murmurs rippled through the audience.

"Finally, ladies and gentlemen, the province will prove beyond reasonable doubt that the defendant's hatred was the reason that Kwame John and his accomplice murdered Dwight in cold blood with malice aforethought. Thank you." He sat down.

I stood still and silent, moved to tears. Why should I suffer for a crime I did not commit? Where was my friend, Faya? I asked myself. It was my lawyer's turn to make his statement. He stood up and walked towards the jury, stopping a few metres from the jury box.

"Ladies and gentlemen of the jury, on June 3, 2003 a young man lost his life. Now the prosecution will have you believe that the defendant was responsible. But there is no scintilla of credible evidence to support this desperate accusation. The defence will present evidence to show that the defendant could not have had and indeed had no hand in the death of Dwight Longman. The defence will show clearly that the case of the prosecution against the defendant is based entirely on suspicion. Now suspicion is no substitute for hard evidence. There are many gaping holes in the prosecution's story. As a result, it is not possible to come to conclude, beyond reasonable doubt, that my client was responsible for this crime. When you have seen the evidence and heard the witnesses, you will be left with no choice but to return a verdict of not guilty. Thank you."

The prosecution opened its case with Joe Bull, the police officer who intercepted Faya and me, took our money and confiscated our entry permit cards.

"The province calls Joe Bull to the witness box," announced the prosecutor.

Joe entered the witness box and was sworn on the Bible. He stood ramrod stiff. The prosecutor then led him through introductory matters. Joe gave his full name, profession, rank and years on the force.

"Do you know the defendant?" the prosecutor asked him.

"I do. His name is Kwame John, a citizen of Jamaica whom I arrested on June 4, 2003 for his role in the murder of Dwight Longman."

"Please tell the court what happened that day," said the prosecutor.

"The previous day, I was on foot patrol in the area at about 7 p.m. Darkness had fallen so I put on my flashlight. When I got to an alley in the neighbourhood I saw somebody sprawled out on the grass. He was immobile. I noticed that his fly was open and the ground was damp. I surmised that he had been urinating. There was a trickle of blood on the side of his mouth. I checked his pulse. I felt nothing. I could tell that he was dead. I then searched the scene and recovered a baseball club and two photo IDs. One was in the name of Faya

Bourne. The other was in the name of Kwame John; and the picture in it bore true resemblance to the accused."

In the dock where I was, I suddenly pitched forward as if someone had pushed me. I made an attempt to say something but the words could not come out of my mouth. My throat felt like sandpaper. Macmillan gave me an angry stare. I started shivering. The shivers led to a convulsion. Clinton Greene rushed to help me. Macmillan raised her voice: "This court is adjourned for forty-five minutes."

After the short recess, I was brought back into the courtroom. My panic seizure had passed. Macmillan gave the floor to Dave Rogers, the prosecutor. Rogers turned to Joe Bull, the police officer: "You testified that you conducted a search of the crime area and found a club and Kwame's photo ID."

"Yes, Your Honour," said Joe.

Rogers moved over to the evidence cart, grabbed two sealed transparent bags and handed them to Joe. "Please tell the court what these are."

Joe held them up so that the jury could see.

"These are the photo IDs I found at the crime scene," said Joe. "This one belongs to Faya Bourne while this other one belongs to Kwame John, the accused."

"Your Honour, I hereby apply to tender these as exhibits," Rogers said and sat down.

"Any objection from the defence?" asked the judge.

Green got to his feet slowly. "None, Your Honour," he said and sat down.

"Very well," said the judge. "Exhibits P1 and P2."

The clerk stepped forward and collected the exhibits for labelling. Rogers went to the evidence cart and picked up another sealed transparent bag. I could see that he was enjoying himself. The noose was tightening around my neck.

"Officer Joe, do you recognize this?" he asked, holding up a club.

"I do, Your Honour. It's the club that I found by the side of the victim, Dwight Longman," he said.

"Your Honour, I apply to tender this as an exhibit in this case," Rogers said.

"No objection, Your Honour," Greene said quickly, halfway out of his seat.

The judge gave him a curious look. My heart pounded wildly. Does my lawyer know what he is doing? I wondered.

"Exhibit P3," announced the judge.

Once again the clerk stepped forward and collected it.

"Officer Joe, what did you do with the exhibits?" asked Rogers.

"Your Honour, I turned them over to the lab technicians at the Woodstock Police Department," answered Joe.

"Officer Joe, in your considerable experience on the police force, can you tell the jury what really happened that day?" asked Rogers.

"The accused must have gone in search of the victim and found him at the alley where he was urinating. He went up behind him and clubbed him to death," answered Joe.

"Do you know his motive for killing Dwight Longman?"

"Yes, Your Honour. I do. Following the arrest of the accused, I obtained a statement from him under caution in which he admitted knowing the victim. The victim had lent the accused his social security number for valuable consideration to enable the accused secure employment. The accused was bitter when he did not get a job after Dwight Longman had caused him to part with money."

"Your Honour, I seek to tender the statement as an exhibit in this case."

"Any objection from the defence?" the judge asked.

"None, Your Honour," Greene said.

"Exhibit P4," the judge said, admitting the exhibit into evidence.

"Thank you, Officer Joe. Your Honour, that is all for the witness," Rogers said." Then he turned to my lawyer. "Your witness."

"Any cross-examination?" asked the judge.

"Yes, Your Honour," said my lawyer, already on his feet. "Officer Joe, when was the first time you ever met or talked to the defendant?" asked Greene.

"It was the morning after the murder," answered Joe.

"Could you tell the jury why you met with the accused?"

"I went to arrest him."

"Why?"

"Because of his photo ID that I found by the victim's body."

"After the arrest, did you obtain a warrant to search his home?"

"Yes, I did."

"Did you conduct a search pursuant to that warrant?"

"We did."

"When did you conduct the search?"

"We conducted the search on the day we arrested the accused."

"Did you find anything during the search?"

"No, Your Honour."

"Officer Joe, where do you normally keep your photo ID?"

Joe gave Greene a puzzled look. "Inside my wallet," he said.

"And where do you keep your wallet?"

"I keep it in my pocket."

"In which one of your pockets do you keep it?"

"I keep it in my back pocket."

"And do you always button up that pocket?"

The police officer stared at Greene without replying.

"Do you or do you not?"

"I always button it up," he answered reluctantly.

"When the accused was searched, do you recall if he had a wallet?"

The police officer thought about this for a while before replying. "No."

"So, what kind of haste would you have been in for your wallet to drop from your back pocket?"

"I don't know."

"Did you find any wallet at the crime scene?"

"No, Your Honour."

"So what you are saying is that the photo IDs somehow managed to wriggle their way out of their wallets and fell off?"

I saw the trap my lawyer had led Joe into. If Joe said yes, he would look less and less credible before the jury. If he said no, he was effectively saying that there was an alternative and definitely more innocent explanation as to how my photo ID got to the crime scene. My respect for Mr. Greene grew.

"Please answer the question," Greene said.

Joe gave Greene a quizzical glance. "I don't know," he said.

"Hmm," Greene said cryptically. "This photo ID, Officer Joe, did you check it for any fingerprints?"

"No," Joe answered slowly.

"Officer Joe, on July 18, 2001, you were assaulted while trying to arrest a man. Is that correct?"

"Yes, Your Honour."

"In fact, the man bit off a chunk of your right ear and ground it into the dust to make it impossible for you to get it stitched back."

"Yes, Your Honour."

"Understandably, you were quite upset."

"I was, Your Honour."

"You still bear the mark of the mutilation?"

"Yes, Your Honour."

"The man was black, and a Jamaican – like the accused in this case."

"Yes, Your Honour."

"You don't like blacks, do you?"

"I am not a racist, Your Honour!" Joe said hotly.

"Funny that you should mention the word. Since the incident, five blacks have reported you to your department for extortion, molestation and harassment."

"Yes, but those reports were investigated and found to be unfounded."

"That is because in each case, it was only their word against yours. There was no additional evidence. Is that not so?"

Joe shifted uncomfortably where he stood. "I don't know."

"Is it not true, Officer Joe, that in all those cases, the complainants alleged that you confiscated their photo IDs and let it be known that you do not like the Canadian government's policy of accepting immigrants?"

"Like I had said, those complaints were found to lack merit."

"That is not the answer to my question, Officer. My question is: were those allegations made at all – as unfounded as they might have turned out to be?"

"Yes, Your Honour. They made those allegations."

"Now let us talk about the club you found at the murder scene. Did you lift any fingerprints off it?"

"Yes, Your Honour. We lifted three sets of prints off the club."

"Let me guess. One of the sets matches your fingerprints– but none matches those of my client, the accused."

"Yes, Your Honour."

Greene looked at the witness for several long seconds. "Officer Joe, did you kill Dwight Longman?"

"No, Your Honour!"

He turned to the judge. "Your Honour, that is all for the witness."

"Any re-examination?" the judge asked.

Rogers got to his feet thoughtfully. "No, Your Honour," he said.

"Next witness!" the judge called.

Rogers stood up. "The Crown calls Dr. Steve Williams."

A bespectacled and bookish-looking middle-aged man strode into the witness box. Rogers led him in evidence to state his credentials, establish that he was a pathologist and that he had practiced his craft for twenty-five years. Then he tendered him as an expert.

"Dr. Williams, you conducted an autopsy on the body of Dwight Longman, did you not?"

"Yes, I did, Your Honour," he answered.

"Please tell the court your findings."

"A single blow was delivered with a blunt object to the occipital bone of the victim. Death was almost instantaneous. The occipital region carries the circuitry for respiration and heart rate. And once the connection was severed by the blow, death followed."

"Could the blunt object that delivered the blow have been a club?"

"It is very likely, Your Honour. My examination of the club found at the crime scene revealed that a portion of the head of the club is slightly faded consistently with contact with a hard object such as the skull. I also found a few strands of hair on it. Tests conducted on the hair show that they are from the victim."

"Dr. Stevens, is it your evidence that the club is the murder weapon?"

"Yes, Your Honour. It is indeed."

"Thank you, sir. Your Honour, that is all for the witness."

"Any cross-examination?" Justice Macmillan asked.

"No, Your Honour," Greene answered, already on his feet.

"The witness may step down," the judge said. Dr. Stevens stepped down and walked slowly back to his seat in the gallery. "Does the crown have any other witnesses?" she asked.

Rogers stood up. "No, Your Honour. The Crown rests."

The judge looked at her watch. "The court is adjourned for two hours. We will reconvene after lunch." She rose and went into her chambers.

⚔ ⚔ ⚔

When the court resumed, the defence, led by Clinton Greene, opened its case. He had decided that I wouldn't testify for fear that I might implicate myself especially considering that I was present when Faya struck the killer blow. He also decided not to call any expert witness to counter Dr. Stevens, assuring me that the medical examiner's testimony was quite harmless: he had not tied me in any way to the murder.

"The defence calls Jonathan Dwyer," he announced.

A middle-aged man in a dark suit and tie stepped into the witness box. He introduced himself as an auditor and proceeded to give his evidence.

"I was standing on the balcony of my house on June 3, 2003. I remember the date because I had just had an appointment with my dentist. I must have been on the balcony for about five minutes when I saw Officer Joe. He has been patrolling the area for the past year or so. So I know him. He stopped two black young men who were going in the opposite direction. And when the accused was arrested, I immediately recognized him as one of the two young men I saw that day with Officer Joe. I couldn't clearly hear what they talked about but I saw them dip their hands in their pockets, fish out their wallets, empty their contents and hand them over to Officer Joe."

"Did the officer return these items to the men?"

"No, Your Honour. He walked away and told them to get lost."

"Thank you, Mr. Dwyer. Your Honour, that is all for the witness."

"Any cross-examination?" the judge asked.

Rogers sprang to his feet. "Yes, Your Honour." He turned to the witness. "Mr. Dwyer, you told this court that, from where you were on the balcony, you could not hear what transpired between the two black men and Officer Joe."

"No, Your Honour, I indeed did not hear them. But the officer accompanied his words with gesticulation. And when he gestured for them to leave, it was unmistakable."

"Mr. Dwyer, I put it to you that you did not see what the young men allegedly handed over to Officer Joe!"

"Your Honour, I have a good idea what they handed over. When the beam of the flashlight hit the items. I could tell that they were some sort of laminated IDs. As for the rest of the items, I believe in my gut that they were dollar notes."

There was a murmur in the jury box. The jurors were taking notes. Rogers seemed to run out of questions. He turned to the presiding judge. "Your Honour, that is all for the witness," he said.

"Defence counsel, any re-examination?" the judge asked.

"None, your honour," said Greene.

"Very well," said Justice Macmillan. "You may step down, Mr. Dwyer. Defence counsel, any other witness?"

"No, Your Honour. The defence rests," Greene said.

"The court is adjourned to tomorrow for closing addresses," the judge said.

⌘ ⌘ ⌘

The next day, the prosecutor was the first to address the jury.

"Ladies and gentlemen of the jury, you have heard the witnesses and seen the evidence. It has been established in evidence that the accused had an axe to grind with the victim. He lost money in an attempt to secure employment. He got mad. And he got even. Moreover, he has no alibi. And it is not enough that his partner in crime is still at large. Under our criminal law, he is a principal offender – even if he did not wield the club. In the circumstance, there is only one verdict you are to deliver in this case: guilty."

Then it was my counsel's turn to address the jury.

"Ladies and gentlemen, you have heard the evidence. My client is innocent. The case that the prosecution has made against him is ridiculous. Firstly, the fingerprints found on the murder weapon were not those of my client. Secondly, the photo ID could not have fallen from the wallet of my client. It was planted at the crime scene – by a man who has an axe to grind with black people, a man who lied that he had never met the accused prior to the arrest of the accused when he had in fact met him, extorted money from the accused and his friend and seized their photo IDs. The prosecution has clearly not discharged its burden in this case – that of proving the guilt of the accused beyond reasonable doubt. And the doubt that lingers as to guilt of the accused must be resolved in favour of my client. I urge you to return with a verdict that is fair and just: not guilty. Thank you."

As if spurred on by an extraordinary force, I burst into tears, screaming at the top of my voice, "I'm not guilty, I'm innocent! My mother is dying of cancer! Please, help me, somebody, help me!" An intense pain struck my back, followed by a feeling of dizziness. The thought of solitary confinement in prison shook me badly, like the threat of Armageddon.

"Calm down," Greene told me sharply.

Justice Macmillan looked at me with a stern expression. She adjourned the case to enable the jury retire to deliberate on the case.

✵ ✵ ✵

The time was now 3 p.m. I was nervous as I sat beside my lawyer and waited. We were in a restaurant near the court. But I could not eat – even though I had not had lunch. About an hour later, the court clerk rang my lawyer on his cell phone.

"The jury has reached a verdict?" I heard my lawyer ask. And then he turned to me. "Let's go back to court."

My heart was pounding, my palms clammy with sweat. I would know in the next few minutes whether I would walk out of the court-room a free man or become a permanent guest of the province.

Shortly after, the court was called into session, and the jurors filed into the jury box.

"Madam Harper, has the jury arrived at an unanimous verdict?" Justice Macmillan asked.

"We have, Your Honour," said the woman.

I became overwhelmed with anxiety, feeling like a raindrop in a storm. I saw somebody in the audience that resembled my mother. Paralyzed by terror, I blinked to make sure, only to realize that it was a hallucination. I must have been blinded by grief. The silence in the courtroom was horrible, spiced up only by my throbbing head.

"In the matter of the Crown against Kwame John on the charge of murder, we the jury find the accused . . . not guilty."

"The accused is free to go," said Justice Macmillan.

I stood perplexed for a long spell, trying to come to grips with the news I had just received. I smiled radiantly, intoxicated with excite-ment and relief. I felt like eating my favourite dish of beans, oxtail and rice. As quick as a flash, the song entitled *Now That We've Found Love* flooded my mind. Greene came over and shook my hand, with victory dancing in his eyes.

After my acquittal, I ceased being a neophyte found wanting of Canadian experience. I was no longer the uncertain and homesick migrant. I decided to forgive all those who have trespassed against me and my ancestors, even the slave traders of the sixteenth to nine-teenth centuries. I became my own hero by mustering courage to request Greene's assistance in my search for a job. My dream of em-ployment was realized when he offered to hire me in his farm. After working for two weeks, I told Greene about my ailing mother, and that I would like to have an advance of wages which he readily gave me. But my mother passed away a day before I sent the money to her. In the weeks that followed, I learnt that Faya was arrested while trying to sneak out of Canada to Jamaica.

5

Polygamy

The sudden alteration of circumstances which changed Saratou's life started one morning in the season of harmattan, at the hour when darkness slowly gave way to light. Rays of sunlight were penetrating through the dew and Freetown was turning on its side, trying to wake up from its deep slumber. The first cock-crow perturbed the quiet of dawn, echoing through Saratou's neighbourhood. The birds had started their dawn chorus, getting ready to welcome the rising tropical sun. The leaves on the branches of trees danced gently in the cool morning breeze as if anxious to bathe in the approaching sunlight. Dogs suddenly stopped their nocturnal howling and barking, like a vehicle brought to an abrupt stop. The sound of pestles pounding foodstuff in mortars and the passionate chants of the muezzin roused Muslims to prayer.

In a shed which served as a kitchen, Saratou bent down low to add more firewood to the fire under a big pot of boiling rice. She squinted against the smoke and brushed her plaited long black hair out of her watery eyes. From a distance she could have been mistaken for a full-figured nineteen-year old. Close up, the lines on her dark-complexioned face showed she was in her early thirties, a troubled woman. Saratou's figure sent the eyes of men darting wherever she walked. She had sensuous lips and large sparkling eyes that were as clear as stars. Her cheeks were slightly plump and dimpled, her eyebrows dark and silky. Her full breasts were the envy of her peers.

Saratou's husband Hamidou did not share that fascination. On several occasions he had threatened to divorce her if she could not bear a child. But she was determined to stay. There was not much she could do except being patient with the hope that one day her marriage situation would improve. Besides, the marriage was arranged by Fatimah, her mother, and Juldeh, her polygamous step-father. Her dislike for this arranged marriage had deteriorated the relationship between Saratou and her parents. She knew that Fatimah's twenty-year marriage was not a happy one. She thought that Juldeh's, like Hamidou's, marital practices were very unfair to her mother. Both women had no social life outside domestic chores. Saratou knew that if it was not for her parent's insistence, she would have divorced her sixty-four year-old husband.

Bintou, Hamidou's first wife, emerged from the house. She had neither washed her face nor brushed her teeth. Saratou was surprised to see her standing in front of the kitchen entrance so early in the morning.

"Good morning, Bintou," Saratou said, stooping to stoke the fire.

"Keep your greetings to yourself," Bintou lashed out at her. "Why would you be married to an old man like Hamidou if not for money?" she said, in heavily accented Krio interspersed with broken French phrases. Bintou had worked as a maid with a French family in Guinea many years ago. She liked to be called La Belle – the beautiful one. Perhaps she has been beautiful once but now in her late forties, it was difficult to see any kennel of beauty in her. She was full of bitterness and hatred. It was even rumoured that she was bewitching Saratou from conceiving children. They whispered that she was the type of woman who would perform her five daily prayers while practising sorcery.

"I'm not married to Hamidou for money. I'll love to bear his children."

"Damn liar! Why don't you go find another man and leave mine alone?" continued the dark-complexioned, medium height woman. Their voices rose and jarred and vied for dominance but that of Bintou radiated more trouble.

"He's my husband," Saratou affirmed, a momentary glint of feminine consciousness appearing in her eyes before her expression turned sombre. "From all accounts you're bewitching me."

"Yes, I am," La Belle whispered, taken aback by Saratou's boldness in the face of her bitterness. "In fact, I want you dead —," she struggled against a fresh wave of anger, "— as dead as a Dodo bird."

"Oh, I see. So, are you the cause of my infertility?"

"Are you asking or telling me?"

"I'm asking you" said Saratou.

"Now, listen, you dummy. You'll never get happiness in this marriage as long as I'm alive."

"Why do you hate me? Why, Bintou?"

"Because, since you entered this house three years ago, Hamidou's love for me died."

"But that's not my fault."

"It's your fault. Tell me, am I frail-looking? Don't you think I want to be loved by him?"

"Talk to him about it. He is your husband."

"You're a mere barren bitch! How dare you talk to me like that?"

Saratou's expression darkened. Every now and then, Bintou had to remind her about her infertility. Not a single day passed that

Saratou did not regret marrying Hamidou. In moments like this, she wondered if fate would ever stop conspiring to deny her from having a child.

Saratou continued with her cooking while Bintou stood menacingly over her.

"I said talk to your husband about it," she said dismissively, brushing past Bintou in the kitchen entrance to fetch more firewood beside the shed. Bintou followed her furiously. Before she knew what was happening, Bintou started beating her head, chest and back with a cane.

"Unruly bitch," Bintou cursed, while Saratou tried to protect herself from the beating.

Once more, the cane descended on Saratou's head and she fell down. The pain was excruciating. Bright stars twinkled in her eyes. Her head bled and throbbed.

"I'll teach you a lesson, you cock of a woman," Bintou yelled, bending down to pick up the cane that had fallen from her grip.

Saratou braced herself and grabbed the cane lying next to her on the ground. She mustered her ebbing strength to stand up and defend herself. Before Bintou could regain her position, Saratou started lashing at her with the cane. The cane landed on its fat side first, then on its thin side, fat side, thin side, in rhythm with Saratou's swinging. With Bintou's relentless screams echoing in her ears, Saratou whipped Bintou's shoulders, upper back, lower back, rump, and the back of her thighs. The cane was cutting her skin open, drawing droplets of blood. Still Saratou continued to lash Bintou who screamed and cried out for help. After a while, all that could be heard from Bintou's clenched teeth were horrible grunts. Her helpless body folded and crumpled to the ground. Bintou lay motionless.

A cock's crow broke the chilly silence as if to report the assault that had just been committed. Saratou felt cold sweat running down her face. She could barely swallow. Terror-stricken, and too frightened to move, she dropped the cane. She looked with horror at Bintou's still figure lying on the ground. What if she has died, what would she do? Run away? Beg for mercy? Commit suicide or serve a prison sentence for murder? She thought about the inhumane conditions she had heard about at the infamous Pademba Road Prisons, otherwise called Tanganyika – stories of rape, torture, hunger, filth, disease and over-crowding. She shuddered.

Then, Hamidou, the husband of the two women, came out at top speed. He was a pious Muslim who strictly followed the tenets of his Islamic faith. He was relatively wealthy and always wore a white ankle-length robe. A short, pudgy, and very nervous man, Hamidou was referred to as Mr. White because of his love for white robes. He did not just *wear* his clothes — he hid inside them. He never wore shoes, only sandals or slippers. His receding gray hair was always neatly trimmed, and his fat, wrinkled head always darted about like a radar blip on his neck. He liked pacing the balcony of his two-story home in a perpetual motion of twitching, fidgeting, and twiddling. In the space of a minute, he would wrinkle his broad nose, scratch his plump chin, shrug his shoulders, straighten his robe, and glance at his watch to check the times for prayers. As he spoke in his lackadaisical drawl, he would glance at the ceiling, inspect his knuckles, and check the furniture for dust. At home, when a conversation with someone was over, he would dash back into his bedroom like a frightened bunny, probably wishing that he could lock himself in there forever.

"What have you done? Are you crazy, Saratou?" Hamidou shouted, grabbing Bintou's arm to check her pulse.

"I didn't mean to do it, I'm so sorry," she muttered and started sobbing uncontrollably.

He pounced on her, seized her by the sleeve of her cotton blouse and flung her backwards. She uttered a cry of pain as she fell on the ground.

"Get up!" he roared and gave her a merciless kick on her side. He had forgotten Saratou as the sight of Bintou's helpless body made his heart flutter with fear and anger.

Slowly, Saratou stood up. Her chest was swollen with hate and her eyes reflected murder. She shrugged and made a face. She was sore at him, and would not get over it for now.

"Enough is enough, and I'm not taking another single minute of this!" Saratou screamed. She suddenly striped off her apron and bolted away in great frenzy.

"Listen, if you step out of my compound, consider our marriage over!" shouted Hamidou. He wanted to quarrel with her. Even though he was raving mad, she was determined not to remain that humble unglamorous wife who kept house. This was her day, she gloried in it, and wanted to make it a resounding success.

"Let it be, it's over for us!" she replied furiously and gave him a reproving glance. She walked away grumbling, "I want to bear a child and all I get instead is molestation."

She had seen a flicker of something in the depths of his brown eyes. Maybe anger, maybe fear. She couldn't be sure. And before he had made up his mind, she headed for her bedroom, grabbed her suitcase, the meagre sum of money she had saved, and headed for Cline Town Wharf.

⚔ ⚔ ⚔

The morning was still and warm, promising a day of sunshine, as Saratou sat with other passengers in the *Redeemer*, the boat that would take her across the river to Targrin, where she planned to consult a Pastor Isaiah, the man of God she believed would cure her infertility. As the boat rolled on her moorings, the rich scent of the sea engulfed Saratou. Her leather slippers, unsuitable for the trip, were already wet and cold on her feet. She had been too anxious about the prospect of meeting Pastor Isaiah to think about the shoes she wore.

Saratou shuddered when she recalled the sight of Bintou's still figure lying on the floor. *Was she dead?* She continued to wonder. She remembered with particular vividness when Hamidou came rushing to the scene where the conflict occurred between herself and Bintou. She thanked God for having saved some money for a day like this when she was able to pay her passage on the open motorized boat. Before now, she had neither been on board a boat nor crossed the wide expanse of water that hopefully would separate her from the heinous act she had committed. The sun began to climb high in the sky and the air slowly became heavy with humidity. From a buoy, a kingfisher trilled her song then darted out across the sea, chased by four noisy seagulls.

The *Redeemer* was born a fishing boat. Just about three years old, she was a simple twenty-two feet of mahogany from the upward sweep of her bow to her stern. At the helm was a fair-complexioned, short, small-boned young man of about thirty years of age whose eyes darted left and right as if looking for something to steal.

"Are you heading for Targrin or Mahera?" the young man asked Saratou.

"Targrin," she replied.

"You looked scared, madam."

"Yes, I am. I've never travelled by sea before."

"Relax. You'll be fine."

"But you're over-loading the boat."

"If I don't, would you pay me to take you across alone?"

Saratou resignedly jerked her head, compelling herself to concentrate on the journey at hand. She wondered how experienced he was to be a skipper. She had heard stories of how some boat owners treated their boats with the same care as their families. She had also heard that for some of them, their true delight in sea-faring started at an early age. For others, it was rumoured that in the absence of the owner, the crew sold their catch in far-away fishing villages and either came home empty-handed or without the outboard engine. By the look of things, this skipper didn't seem to be the owner of this boat.

The *Redeemer* was minutes shy of pulling away from the wharf when a pleading cry came from ashore.

"Wait! Please wait!"

A fat woman ran down the wharf, staggering under the weight of an extra-large basket of dried fish that bounced against her head.

"Don't go, please wait for me!" she cried.

One of the crew members took her basket and squeezed it close to Saratou's feet. She dared not open her mouth for fear that she would be overpowered by sickness. Realizing that she was in for a long haul, she drew her shawl tighter around her. Over an hour late, the *Redeemer* was finally released from her line and moved out to sea. She rode low in the waters. The next thirty minutes saw the *Redeemer* covered by fog. The sun was nowhere to be seen. Saratou could not even see the passenger seating next to her. She recalled news of badly-maintained boats sailing at night without lights and capsizing. More frightful reveries passed through her mind in rapid succession. She was abruptly pulled from her thoughts when suddenly the *put-put* of the boat's engine stopped. All she could hear was the crew arguing about something that she could not understand.

"Eh, some of you move to the left-hand side!" shouted someone who sounded like the skipper. But before they could order their stupefied minds to action, the *Redeemer* tipped over and capsized, throwing all overboard. Saratou went underwater in a stunned state. When her head broke the surface, she gasped for fresh air. She fought the waves that rose around her, in an effort to remain afloat. In shallow gasps, she regained her breath, and then heard the echoes of passengers screaming. The *Redeemer* was lying on the water on her side like a paralysed old lady. Seagulls soared noisily around the accident scene.

It was only then that the fog began to disperse creating a sunlit sea. The devastation was breathtaking. Saratou and the others were struggling to hold on to whatever object they could lay their hands on. Her slippers were gone, as was her handbag, and when she felt the weight of her wet jacket dragging her down, she managed to struggle out of it while holding on to an empty five-gallon rubber container. She was trembling uncontrollably both from shock and the chilly waters.

She had no idea how far they were from the shore but suddenly the head of a man appeared. He shouted, "Don't let go that container, and pray in the name of the Lord!"

"I'm Pastor Isaiah," he continued. Saratou, like a woman pulled between fright and delight during childbirth, could not believe her ears. The realization that she was about to drown and the shock of hearing the pastor's name made her sick.

Suddenly, she heard the drone of an engine, and a tug boat materialized out of the dispersing fog. In a short while, she was lifted into the boat by its crew with the help of the pastor. Dripping wet and trembling under the jersey that was given to her, she nevertheless felt relieved. The tugboat made a couple of rounds at the accident scene in an attempt to rescue survivors.

"We'll drop you ashore," the captain said as the boat picked up speed.

While First Aid was being provided to the survivors, Saratou shivered as the wind whipped through her wet hair. Within minutes, the mist thinned to reveal Targrin, a small fishing village on the Bullom peninsula.

⚒ ⚒ ⚒

The tugboat pulled up to the dock and Pastor Isaiah helped Saratou ashore. Immediately, he dropped down on his knees and turned to her and other survivors.

"Let us pray," he asked of them, raising his arms to the sky and closing his eyes. Saratou and others followed suit.

"In the name of our heavenly Father, and the only begotten Son of God, peace and good tidings are the blessings that the gospel brought to this our troubled world. Just a few hours ago, Christ and His angels buoyed us up from the deep sea and brought us ashore with renewed strength and resolute hope. And when God has rescued us may we have the good sense to walk away from sin, and let the past bury the past. If any one of us has made a mistake but we've done our best according to the teachings of the Lord and the governance of the Church to confess it and feel sorrow for it, then trust in God, walk into His light and leave the ashes behind you — Alleluia!"

"Amen!" Saratou and others responded.

In his mid-forties, Pastor Isaiah was a tall and majestic figure depicting spiritual authority. His thin eyebrows and narrow nose gave him a handsome look. He was dark in complexion, compassionate and jovial. When he walked, his heels barely touched the ground. He walked as if ready to fly. Pastor Isaiah was not an ordinary man of God. Although he looked simple, many considered him a messiah who performed wonders for the sick and suffering. He also exorcised witches and wizards. Praises for his miracles could be heard on the lips of the young and old. People from all over the country and beyond came to visit the Isaiah Healing Church where he offered prayers on their behalf for prosperity, good health, and fertility. For many, the pastor was as good a man as gold.

Pastor Isaiah took Saratou to his church where she was accommodated with other women in an adjoining building in the church's compound. Her joy could not be expressed in words. After a couple of days, the pastor requested an interview in his office with her. When she appeared his breath caught in his throat. He was impressed by her beauty.

"So what's your problem?" he asked. The question caught her unawares and at first rendered her speechless. After a brief while she started speaking slowly, with studied calm and a broad smile on her face. Her words came as though spurred by an internal force.

"I am barren and I would like you to pray for me to bear children."

"My dear sister-in-Christ, it would be my pleasure."

"Thank you pastor for accepting to relieve me of the pain and stigma I now face."

"Our meeting may appear to be accidental but it's destined by God."

"I believe so too, pastor."

"By the grace of God, our prayers will be accepted thereby bringing an end to your chastisement and ostracism."

"Pastor, I'm at your command."

"To begin the healing process, you'll fast for thirty days from dawn to dusk, read the Book of Psalms several times a day, and give alms to the poor. You'll perform spiritual bathing before breaking your fast with fruits, vegetables and water."

"Yes, pastor, I'll do as you say."

"We'll not ask the Lord why you were denied the joys of motherhood even though you were blessed with a striking appearance."

"Pastor, I'll do anything you say, even allow you to savour my beauty," she called out in desperation.

Her large sparkling eyes blinked dreamily, wondering if the pastor truly meant his remarks about her appearance or if she had made a mistake by giving the pastor an open invitation. What a nerve she had! She felt as guilty as sin.

"I'll not do such a thing, my dear sister-in-Christ, for only God will provide for me." It made him angry to detect unsteadiness in his voice when he spoke. How indiscreet and indecorous of her to think the unthinkable! Since when could Pastor Isaiah of all people be seduced by a female worshipper? But as he looked at Saratou he found that his throat went dry, his heartbeat became rapid and he was filled with physical desire for her. *Oh Lord, lead me away from this temptation,* he prayed silently.

"I'm sorry pastor if I've annoyed you," she said, aware of her effect on the pastor.

"It's all right, it's all right." He bit his nails and cursed himself.

"I'm sorry to have mentioned that, pastor," Saratou said, trying to keep her tone casual.

"It's all right," he said again, but she heard him sigh softly.

Pastor Isaiah closed his eyes, raised his hands as if in prayers, and recalled how he had turned down the requests of women who had offered their naked bodies to him.

⁂ ⁂ ⁂

Before the end of a fortnight, rumour had it that the pastor was having an affair with Saratou. Whenever two or three gathered together in the church compound, the very first question was about the rumour: Could you believe it? Did you know that Pastor Isaiah is sleeping with Saratou? There were some who, like the biblical Thomas, doubted the rumour. Those who claimed to be in the know asserted that the pastor was annoyed about the rumour and that much of his annoyance was directed at Saratou.

Finally, she approached the pastor and begged for mercy swearing that since she arrived in the church compound, she had never discussed the pastor with anybody. Saratou's attempt to dispel the pastor's wrath by explaining that she did not even know how the rumour came about made matters worse. He scolded her for her lack of discretion and wisdom.

Was she implying that she had no idea of the source of this horrible rumour when she was the very serpent that tried to seduce him? Why had she been such a fool to have given the opportunity to others to make this rumour a subject of heated debate? How was he going to rectify this problem in order to maintain his reputation? Damn it! He swore, and momentarily remembered that he was a man of God who should not swear.

For some days, Pastor Isaiah would not receive Saratou, who became so worried that she took steps to stave off his burning anger. She began by pleading with other worshippers, especially women, to desist from spreading the rumour. While some promised to keep their mouths shut, others simply ignored her.

On the twenty-first day of her fasting and praying, a small hornlike object was invoked spiritually by Pastor Isaiah and Saratou vomited it out in the presence of the congregation. According to him, if she had gone for a surgical operation in her quest for a baby, she would have died. By the final day of her fasting and praying her appetite for food and drink increased. She began to feel healthier. Pastor Isaiah informed her that he had broken the spell cast on her by Bintou, whom he branded a witch.

Shortly afterwards, Saratou was astounded to receive a marriage proposal from the pastor on condition that she divorced Hamidou and converted to Christianity.

"Pastor, thank you so much for your help and consider me divorced from Hamidou," she said.

"However, we must keep your parents and ex-husband informed."

"That's fine with me."

"All right, I'll invite your parents to my church."

⚒ ⚒ ⚒

A couple of days later, the pastor and Saratou received Fatimah and Juldeh. The pastor made his marriage intention known to Saratou's parents. He told them about the importance of her being baptized and converted to Christianity after being cured in the name of the Lord and saviour Jesus Christ.

"A woman professes the religion of her husband," said Juldeh who, like his wife, willingly agreed. Fatimah then informed them that Bintou was seriously ill. She explained how Bintou may even die as she had confessed to being a witch.

"I witnessed her saying that through witchcraft, she turned her left hand into a knife, opened your womb and placed a horn in there to make you barren," sobbed Fatimah.

"Oh, my God," cried Saratou.

"That horn is no longer in her," said the pastor.

"That's true, mama. By God's grace, I was able to vomit it."

"Thank God, and thank you, pastor," said Fatimah.

"It's my duty," Pastor Isaiah replied humbly.

"Bintou said that she was given the witchcraft spirit by her maternal grandmother at the age of seven," continued Fatimah.

"From the onset I knew something was wrong in that marriage," said Saratou.

"As to how she went out to the witches' coven, Bintou said she would spiritually put her household to sleep, turn into smoke and pass under the door of the room. Once outside, she would turn into a bat and fly away," concluded Fatimah.

❌ ❌ ❌

The night before Saratou's baptism and marriage ceremonies, which were to take place the same day, the drizzling rain became a heavy downpour. Lightning was followed by thunder. A moaning and crashing sound came from swinging and breaking trees and hedgerows as the wind and the rain beat the leaves and the branches.

The morning was so gloomy Saratou and Pastor Isaiah dreaded the day would not break into existence. The rain had stopped though. The air was mild and cool, and a welcoming heat seeped from the expectant ground to their hearts. This was their day as the church's congregation emptied themselves into the compound. Their cheers resonated like a great breaking of trees falling on sludge.

It was a delightful ceremony of colours as everybody was dressed in beautiful traditional fabrics. The compound was decorated with flamboyant wraps made from colourful silk. The tables and chairs were covered with gold-coloured fabric, and the floral display had different colours of roses. The food, music, dance, and coloured balloons gave style to the celebration.

In the months that followed, Pastor Isaiah showed Saratou so much love that she began to realize how much Hamidou's polygamous marital practice had deprived her of love and bliss. She began to develop compassion for Fatimah, who has been married to her polygamous step-father for twenty years. Slowly, her compassion led to improved relationships between mother and daughter. As time went by, Saratou realized that her dream of bearing a child was verging on reality. When she became pregnant, the news swept like angry flames in the community. After nine months, Saratou gave birth to a bouncing baby girl and lived happily ever after with Pastor Isaiah.

6

Murder In Koidu Town

Koidu Town: a chaotic diamond-mining town hungry for profit and pleasure; a town prodigal of hustlers. The lights in the town's *Capitol* cinema hall had just been turned off. It was 8 p.m. on Palm Sunday, 1969. The film, *Seven Slaves against Rome*, was about to start. The lady stared at the empty balcony seat beside her and waited.

Sammy Koedoyoma, in his mid-forties, was not what most people would call handsome. He was a dark, tall and skinny man with a leanly muscled build. Sammy looked just like Kipchoge Keino, the Kenyan Olympic athlete, although less handsome than Kipchoge. Sammy had a goatee, and he wore sun glasses even at night. There was an air of destitution about him, an air of being out of place. He was a kind, loving person; also a good father. People who knew him in Koidu Town thought the world of him. It was uncharacteristic. Sammy had never been late for an appointment before. Even when he was drunk you could set your timepiece by him.

When he arrived about forty minutes later, Sammy's explanation to the lady for not being on time was as clear as mud: He had been delayed by one Nadia Ahmed who wanted to know the whereabouts of Salwa. Both in their early fifties, Nadia and Salwa were women whose fathers were of Lebanese origin, and they knew each other.

Salwa cleared her throat nervously like a girl about to ask her parents for money.

"You know what someone told me once?" Salwa asked Sammy.

"What's that?" Sammy inquired, a veiled curiosity reflecting in his eyes.

"It seems psycho, but a man said you know a contract killer."

"Who said that?"

"I don't know," she said. "Maybe it was one of the store keepers. What does it matter who?"

"He must have been talking about Komba," Sammy said.

"Komba?"

"Komba Sonda. He is a friend of mine. Whoever told you that must have meant Komba."

"Who is he?"

"He works at the diamond mines in the outskirts of Koidu town."

"So would he?" Salwa asked.

"You mean actually kill a person?"

"Yes. Would he do it?"

Suddenly the curiosity ceased to be veiled. The interest in Sammy's eyes leaped up.

"Not Komba, no. Komba's a nice man."

"He is not shady?"

"No. I believe he does illicit mining but he's cool. He would never do anything like homicide."

"So it's not true?" Salwa said. "He's not a contract killer?"

"A contract killer? My God, no. Not Komba. He's a jester. He always says to me, "Sammy, if you need a killer, let me know.""

"He meant he would kill for money?"

"Yes, but he's only joking."

"Bullshit," Salwa said.

"Are you thinking about getting rid of someone?"

There was a momentary hesitation on Salwa's part and then she laid a hand on his arm and drew him forward.

"Forget it," Salwa snapped.

They sat in silence for a while, watching the film, as a battle raged between the seven slaves and Rome. The audience grew rowdy. Sammy was slowly becoming nauseated by the stench of cigarette smoke in the cinema hall. Alcohol was Sammy's addiction, not cigarettes. As if to aggravate the situation, Salwa lit a cigarette too. A man seating a couple of yards away walked up to borrow Salwa's cigarette lighter.

"Truly, I can't imagine Komba Sonda killing anybody," he said as if to convince himself. "But . . ."

"But what? Salwa cut him short.

A slow and rather peculiar smile twisted Sammy's lips.

"But he might know somebody who would."

The duo left the cinema hall before the end of the film. It was a relief for Sammy as the smell of cigarette smoke hung thickly in the hall. Apparently, they were only there for the rendezvous.

✵ ✵ ✵

Koidu Town was as hot as hell in the month of March. Although rich in diamonds, the town was sorely lacking in basic social amenities. After the unexpected rains the previous night, the town smelled of wet soil and mulch. This prevented Sammy from taking his usual deep morning gulps of air.

Sammy was standing at the edge of an alluvial diamond-mining pit waiting for Komba Sonda to join him. The diamond mines in this area were no different from those in the whole district; whether it was in Yengema, Motema, Tombodu, Jaima-Nimokoro, or Jaima-Sewafe.

There were dozens of impoverished youths sifting through tonnes of sand, mud and dirt in search of diamonds.

Komba Sonda was a big, afro hair-styled man with black side-burns and red eyes. He breathed heavily and smelled of marijuana. His dark-brown narrow face needed a shave. Brown teeth and nicotine-stained fingers made him look unhealthy although he was as strong as an ox.

"Hello, Sammy, what's up?" Komba said, walking up to Sammy, carrying his pick-axe, shovel, and sieve.

"All is well. And you?"

"Well, as you can see, apart from the grueling hours spent in the hot sun mining, all is well."

"Indeed, Komba, it's only to live hand-to-mouth."

"And months into this mad prospecting enterprise of which there seems to be no end in sight," Komba complained, dropping his pick-axe, shovel, and sieve on the ground.

Both men shook hands and patted each other on the shoulder.

"Maybe it's time to find another job, with less copious labour being expended daily."

"But Sammy, you know how things are in this town."

"I know, my friend. Our options for survival are limited."

"The search for diamonds is not absolutely easy. Under the best circumstances, the work is fraught with dangers. There is always the possibility of mudslides, collapsing walls, and drowning," said Komba.

"And illicit miners like you caught in mining concessions are frequently shot and killed."

"As sure as death and taxes, provided you're not killed by sexually transmitted diseases," said Komba, smiling.

"Life out here is so variable. Even though the government can't provide you with jobs, they claim that in the frenetic search for diamond deposits, illicit miners leave the land unsuitable for farming activities, and prone to soil erosion" Sammy pointed out.

"It's all double standard, my friend," said Komba, dismissively. "What about the heavy minerals and chemical products from mining equipment of government mines? These chemicals run off into rivers and pollute our vital water sources."

"Listen, maybe this may be a break-through for you. I'm looking for somebody who would kill for money", Sammy said.

"You must be joking," Komba said, laughing. For a while, he kept on laughing, his eyes were now nothing more than tear-filled incisions. His head shook and his teeth glimmered. He growled and panted and shook his head and hunched his shoulders and still came out of it laughing.

"I'm not joking," Sammy said.

"You mean actually kill a person?" Komba asked as if to confirm his comprehension.

"Yes, a friend of mine needs a contract killer" Sammy replied.

Seeing that Sammy was not joking, Komba said, "I can do it if the money is paid." He then gave Sammy an unwavering gaze, as a sly expression of intense cunning twisted his face.

"Okay, Komba, I'll get back to you after informing my friend, Salwa."

Sammy left the mining vicinity looking as agile as a monkey, and went home. Without fully comprehending the implications of what he was doing, Sammy started acting as a go-between for a hired murder.

✼ ✼ ✼

At an early age, Sammy was deserted by his parents. He grew up with an aunt. At twenty-four Sammy became an alcoholic. At forty he had marital problems which left him with a twenty-two year old son, Augustine. Even though Sammy was drinking heavily, his life seemed to be under control.

He had been a good man but too old for Ahjawkeh, his wife. She had married because he offered security, an income, and a home. There was no passion in the marriage, but she had found joy when Augustine was born. "You're my joy," Ahjawkeh told Sammy, every day and night. She always said until death do us part until that fateful day that she eloped with a rich yet polygamous man.

Sammy was very intelligent and his first job was that of a government representative at the Diamond Mining Company (DIMINCO). Later, he worked as a diamond evaluator in a large firm. But with no wife and a child, he was desperate for money. He stole a diamond from the firm, and he was caught. He did not go to jail, but his agreement with the firm prevented him from ever taking another important position.

He became a bus driver at Nadia Ahmed's Commercial Vehicle Company. There were many women in his life, and all of them treated him like a drunken fool. They fleeced him. Their lies were told with such conviction that they could always fool him. All of these issues became an insurmountable burden on Sammy; hence his addiction to alcohol, and alliance to the wrong group of people.

✖ ✖ ✖

Sammy informed Salwa about Komba's willingness to murder someone for money. So one evening, the trio met at the *Kobassi* restaurant downtown. As dinner was being served, they sat down comfortably and traded small talk. Then out of the blue, Salwa said to the two men, "I've made up my mind. I'm going to tell you her name. I hope I can trust you."

Komba said, "You can trust me. Sammy can attest to that."

"Sammy!" Salwa called out. His eyes were fixed on an invisible horizon. Sammy did not say anything. He turned and stared at her.

"Sammy, can I trust your friend as I trust you?"

As if awaken from a day-dream, Sammy responded, "For sure Salwa you can trust him."

"Nadia Ahmed is her name and she owns the Commercial Vehicle Company," said Salwa pulling gently on her dark flowing hair.

Both men were surprised at the mention of the name but they didn't show it. They knew Nadia Ahmed; one of the richest Lebanese women in Koidu town. Nadia was Sammy's employer. For Salwa to be telling them to get rid of such a person sounded like an abomination. Sammy felt a strong lump in his throat. A few months ago, by no stretch of the imagination could he be seen as acting as a broker for a hired killer, contracted to kill his boss. The surroundings were silent, yet he could sense a strange restlessness beneath.

In the icy stillness her voice was scarcely audible, "I'll pay thirty thousand leones for the job to be done."

Komba said, "That amount is too small madam"

It stopped her. "What do you mean? This is 1969."

The year 1969 in Sierra Leone was associated with women's liberation. It was the year when women made it fashionable to wear tight-fitting trousers and high-heel shoes; a year of false life and high life.

"But this is a big and risky job," Komba said wrinkling his nose.

Salwa's large and round eyes with ink-black irises glinted resentfully. There was not a hint of colour in those eyes, and its long lashes emphasized their hypnotic effect. Her nerves grated with irritation. He saw her anger mounting. She flared up.

"Forget it!" She shouted and stood up. With her tall and slim stature, her olive skin, she could always expect people to obey her, especially black men. Her eyes bored right through Komba and beyond. She pondered, squeezing her heavily-ringed hand. Who was Komba? Where did he get the effrontery to challenge her? She called for the bill and started walking away. Her earrings – big golden loops – dangled in rhythm with her quick footsteps. She looked pale as her beauty had now become a fading illusion.

Once Salwa went into her Mercedes Benz 190 car and drove away, Sammy and Komba looked at each other in a baffled manner. Silently, they walked out of the restaurant and stood outside.

Komba said, "My friend, you know what? Half a man's troubles are caused by women."

A fly buzzed in front of Sammy's face. He swatted it. His mouth was dry, his tongue thick.

"What do you think?" he asked Komba in a voice that was fast descending to a croak.

Dismissively, Komba said, "I'm no longer interested."

With the very air into which he spoke hanging listless as a sheet, Sammy said, "I don't blame you."

"The woman didn't even bargain," said Komba, feeling sick of the sound of his own voice.

"How much were you expecting her to pay you?"

"Fifty thousand leones would have been fine with me."

"Should I let her know?"

"No. It's only a man like you that such a short-tempered and arrogant woman can use. I've already told you that I'm no longer interested", Komba repeated and walked away, leaving Sammy standing tongue-tied.

⚒ ⚒ ⚒

A couple of days later, Salwa was able to convince Sammy that they can kill Nadia Ahmed and make away with her riches. In the grip of greed Salwa asked Sammy to accompany her to the neighbouring state of Liberia to buy a gun. The moment they arrived in Monrovia, Sammy and Salwa were approached by a couple of illegal gun dealers. But none of them could persuade Salwa in terms of price and confidentiality.

Then they met a Lebanese woman in her sixties, a widow whose husband had passed away leaving her a .32 calibre gun. The widow had resolved to sell the gun because one of her sons had attempted to steal it.

When they arrived at the widow's residence, Salwa asked Sammy to wait inside her car while she went indoors. With a cup of coffee at her elbow in the widow's pleasant-smelling and softly lit living room, Salwa bought the gun in Sammy's name without his knowledge. Eighty American dollars was all she paid for it. On that same day, the two travelled back to Koidu Town.

Salwa Abbess was a spoiled, troubled Sierra Leonean - Lebanese woman who was desperately afraid that her father will find out she was into prostitution and robbery. She had never fallen in love with a man who embraced her with passion. Salwa loved her Lebanese father deeply, but he was hardly interested in her perceived failings.

Sierra Leone was not her country. She had been born there but never belonged. She was a half-caste who was not wanted in her native land by either the black Sierra Leoneans or the white Lebanese. She had been born to a Sierra Leonean woman who was her father's housemaid. Apart from Nadia, Salwa did not have one friend who had not run up debts. Driven by one Kono woman, Sia Matturi, Salwa joined the Bondo Society, a women-only secret cult. Salwa had little to show for so many years in Koidu Town. It was time to make some money.

Nadia Ahmed was a pale little creature who was successful but an unlikeable Lebanese businesswoman. She had never been married to any man. She always thought that none was fit enough to put a ring on her finger. But she was a lover of young black men and SUVs. Once upon a time she hated and distrusted these men. But over the years, first hesitantly, then more confidently, she picked the best men, used them, and threw them back into the streets. She bought stolen goods from Salwa and from other miscreants and criminals. Salwa often stole from Nadia, but Nadia always took her back. Unknown to Nadia, Salwa had other buyers of stolen goods. So, the relationship between her and Salwa had become tempestuous.

✠ ✠ ✠

The sun had set when Salwa began to walk the one mile from her house to *Yellow Submarine*, a downtown nightclub. She was due to meet Sammy there at nine o'clock. At this time of the night, the streets were less crowded and not as noisy as during the day. She had avoided driving her car because of the nature of the dubious task ahead. Salwa hurried, keeping to the better-lit streets and being careful to avoid muddy paths and potholes.

Her outfits were always striking. She wore a mauve skirt with a beige-coloured blouse and black tights; the silver buckle on her brown belt matched the silver balls of her earrings.

She walked through darker streets, tightening her grip on the handbag. The town council had promised electric lighting in every main streets leading from Hospital Road right down to the main market, but it had not happened. Not that she cared. Even in a dark lane teeming with pickpockets, Koidu Town was the innermost part of her world. She loved the town. It had given her privilege, the chance to forge her existence, to live on her wits and charisma. This was the town that had attracted her father's people to leave Lebanon in search of diamonds, and seeking refuge from war.

The dark and silent lane gave way suddenly to the noise and glowing light of small Lebanon; electric lighting powered by standby generators. Salwa stepped into a street crowded with people, and quickly entered the *Yellow Submarine*.

Men and women in psychedelic attire lounged against a bar. A haze of cigarette smoke hung over the bunch of people. The floor was packed with tables, and nightclub goers smoking, drinking, and dancing to blaring music. The Congolese song *Si tu bois beaucoup* by Orchestre Zaire Attack was sending people into a frenzy.

Salwa saw Sammy at the near end of the bar and beckoned to him to join her. He noisily gulped down his *Sassman* rum, rose to his feet, and staggered over, muttering to himself. He reached out for a hand shake which she declined. Wearing a black tight-fitting long-sleeved shirt that matched his black bell-bottom trousers, Sammy reeked of cheap alcohol.

"Shall we go?" He asked gently as if not to cause a stir or a ripple.

"Yes, let's go," replied Salwa smacking her vermilion-coloured lips.

They walked out of the nightclub onto a crowded street refreshed by the cool easterly wind. On foot, Salwa and Sammy headed to Nadia's house at the Reservation, not far from the *Yellow Submarine*. As they approached the house they heard a dog barking from the compound. Johnny, the security guard, a tall, dark, strikingly handsome fellow in overalls, met them at the gate. Salwa had a hunch that he must have slept with Nadia. Counting Nadia's father, and the dog, they were the only four living in the six bedroom luxury house. Flashlight in one hand, he appeared surprised to see the two, whom he knew, at that time of night.

Likewise, Salwa was surprised to see Johnny because she learnt from the grapevine that he was supposed to be off duty.

"We had wanted to speak with Nadia, urgently," she said.

Johnny glanced at his wrist watch and shook his head, "It's too late," he said solemnly.

"I know but we were delayed by an unforeseen circumstance."

"Why not come back tomorrow morning?"

Realizing that she cannot break the impasse, she conceded "That's right. See you then."

As Salwa and Sammy were leaving the vicinity, dishearten disheartened, the dog, in a rage, barked and snapped, trying to tug loose from Johnny. She checked inside her handbag to make sure that the .32 calibre gun and bullets were still there.

ℑ ℑ ℑ

Failing to accomplish her mission at Nadia's, Salwa made another appointment with Komba Sonda. They met on the roadside under a baobab tree whose shade is used by the general public. This time, after much deliberation, they finally agreed on a time, a place and a price for the murder. It will take place in Nadia's house at night time for a price of fifty thousand leones.

"To help me do this job, I would like to hire somebody else," said Komba.

"As long as the job is done discreetly," responded Salwa with a coquettish smile at Komba.

She then looked at Sammy, in a cold, sullen, and expectant manner. He was surprisingly quiet.

So for the sake of saying something, Sammy blurted, "Are you nervous to do it all alone?"

"Not that I'm nervous but . . ."

"But what is it?" Sammy interrupted Komba.

"Two heads may be better than one," said Komba.

"Do you mind my asking who this person is?"

"He is called Mbawa "Highway" Gbamanga."

"You mean the notorious Highway?"

"Yes, it's him," Komba responded quietly.

"I don't think so, Komba. That man is a known criminal," said Sammy, glancing at Salwa who stood by the two men seemingly unconcerned.

"Who else do you think can do it?" asked Komba

"Not Highway. Find somebody else," Sammy suggested.

Salwa jumped into the conversation: "I don't care who does the job," she said dismissively.

Like a dog with its tail between its legs, Sammy shuddered and kept quiet. The trio then dispersed.

✵ ✵ ✵

A couple of years ago, Komba Sonda was an unemployed bachelor who wanted to become rich through mining diamonds. He applied for a job in the government mining company in Yengema, not far from Koidu Town, but he was not hired. With pick-axe, shovel, and sieve, he decided to join others in illicit mining. Not too long after that, he was arrested, detained for two months without trial, and released.

Komba went back to illicit mining under the employment of one man by the name of Sahr Mondeh. This man was known to be a ruthless diamond merchant who maltreated his workers. One day, Sahr Mondeh accused Komba of stealing and swallowing a two-carat piece of diamond. Although he denied, yet he was forced to take a purgative after which the diamond was found in his feces. Beaten mercilessly, and left in the street to die, Komba was found by Mbawa "Highway" Gbamanga who took him to the hospital where he later recovered.

Even after his discharge from the hospital, Komba's life was heading miserably to failure and poverty. It was not until Highway initiated him into armed robbery and illicit mining that he saw a brief respite from despair. Nevertheless, he was a gentle, likable man with no criminal record.

In the case of Mbawa "Highway" Gbamanga, he was a notorious contract killer from Freetown with a criminal record. As a child, he experienced abuse, and family dysfunction which created emotional disturbances for him and his siblings.

As one of three boys in the family, Mbawa had two younger brothers. All three of them (Mbawa, Tamba, and Aiah) aged eighteen, seventeen, and sixteen at the time) including their mother, Nana, had legal orders filed against them for breach of the peace.

There was no father present in the home. Two years prior to Mbawa's thirteen birthday, his father had abandoned wife and children and taken up life in Liberia with a widow ten years his senior, leaving a note of adieu on the kerosene powered refrigerator. He had not been seen or heard of since.

Prior to Mbawa's father abandonment, the family was relatively stable, but once the breadwinner of the home left, it became unmanageable for Mbawa's mother. The children not only became unruly and school drop-outs, but they all turned out to be perpetual criminals.

꙳ ꙳ ꙳

As the murder plan unfolded, Sammy became frightened; near to death. One day, he was on the telephone speaking with his son Augustine, who was now living in Makeni Town, when he realized that his limbs were numbed.

"Salwa and I are working on a plan," Sammy said. His voice choked.

"What is it you're working on, papa?

"With time, I'll let you know."

Sammy could not breathe. *This is not happening*, he said to himself as he hung up the telephone. He was a chaotic bag of feelings, truly worried that Nadia was going to be killed. Sammy was afraid that he might be murdered if he told the police, and so he was anxious to have it over with.

The only person that he could confide in was Augustine. In another telephone call to him Sammy said:

"I may become the manager in Nadia's Commercial Vehicle Company."

"Is that right, papa?"

"That's right, my son."

"Has Nadia hinted at it?"

"Yes, she has. And she has even asked me to find her another security guard as she has fired Johnny."

"It looks like money will be coming your way soon."

"Say that again, my son, as we're going to murder Nadia," Sammy said laughing softly.

In a cloud of silence, Augustine became confused. Was his father saying something real or not?

"Papa, have you been drinking?"

"No, I haven't," he lied.

Maybe, this was one of his father's drunken digressions. If his father was saying the truth, he should quit before a consequence worse than death befell him. But he will not. He was stubborn, and determined to make money. Or should he go ahead and inform the police immediately? But he could not as this was his own father who may be having an illusion. The murder was not going to happen, Augustine thought.

On the night of the murder Salwa, Komba, and Mbawa met at Nadia's Commercial Vehicle Company depot. Salwa and Komba drove to Nadia's house. Johnny was absent. They came back at midnight to inform Sammy that they had done the job. They had murdered Nadia.

⌘ ⌘ ⌘

Now that the deed had been done, Sammy and Salwa returned to Nadia's house the next morning. Surrounded by the stench of death, they cleaned up the blood, dragged Nadia's body and that of the dog into a shed attached to the house. It was in this shed that they buried the remains.

Nadia's father, Jamil Ahmed, in his seventies and close to infirmity, lived in an adjoining building on the vast Nadia property. Sammy told him that Nadia had urgently departed to Lebanon on a business trip. On a daily basis, he started bringing meals for Jamil, and taking care of the old man.

The time was early afternoon, and the day was hot. March generally prompted torrents of rain, mocking anyone's hope for the dry season. But this year, the weather was setting itself up to be different. Days of sun in a cloudless sky made the promise of an April and a May during which the ground would scorch, making people drink tons of water.

Salwa and Sammy went to the Commercial Vehicle Company depot. Salwa called all the employees together in an assembly hall. She was standing behind a long table, looking crisp and clean and remarkably fit for a woman her age. At her command, Sammy sat down. She wanted him to feel her sovereignty on the chance that he might think himself her superior. Then, she announced:

"Nadia has gone to Lebanon on business and she would be away for a long time."

A strange quiet ensued, cloaked by a blanket of heat.

"I'll be the boss now, but I won't be around much," she continued, taking a broad glance across the group.

"Sammy Koedoyoma will be the manager of the company," she added as the group whispered, and stared at her quizzically.

The employees doubtfully accepted the idea, though after several weeks, like a stain, rumours began to spread that Nadia was dead. None of the employees paid much attention to this episode as news of the discovery of a big diamond named 'the Star of Sierra Leone' was in the air. It was a discovery that shook the diamond world; one that sparked the greatest mining rush in the history of Koidu Town.

On that same day, Sammy called his son Augustine and said:

"I've been appointed as Manager at Nadia's Commercial Vehicle Company."

"Congratulations, papa!"

"Thank you."

"And what about Nadia and Salwa?"

"Nadia is dead, and Salwa is the new boss."

Augustine could not find words to respond to his father. Then everything changed for him. He started having an emotional breakdown. Apparently, he cannot live with what he knew, and he cannot betray Sammy. From then on, life for Augustine seemed as elusive as wisps of smoke. He started to drink to drown his troubles.

One day, his father told him: "Augustine, it's time for you to face up to your preferences. Either you live with an emotional breakdown, or you put the whole experience behind you and start a new chapter."

Augustine wanted to respond, but Sammy cut him short. "Do you hope you can amend the crimes of the past by agonizing in the present?"

Never yet had father and son been so far and so sorely apart. Sammy was unnerved.

Again, that chaotic bag of feelings washed over Sammy: lethargy, indifference and weightlessness, as if he had been eaten away from inside by termites. For the first time he had a jolt of what it will be like to be old, without desires, aloof to the forthcoming challenges.

Who would confess about a murder crime to him?

Despite being tortured by his knowledge of the murder, and drinking, Sammy remained in control with a heart as hard as a butcher's. He ran the Commercial Vehicle Company. He told the bogus story. And it seemed as if they had gotten away with the crime.

⁂

About twelve weeks later, people became inquisitive though not dismayed about Nadia's absence. Apart from Salwa, Nadia had no close friends or relatives except her father, Jamil. He kept asking questions about her daughter's so-called trip to Lebanon. The murderers had hoped he would die of natural causes. But as Jamil lived on they were getting nervous.

On a Wednesday at mid-morning, Salwa told Sammy: "We'll have to kill Jamil."

"No Salwa, I don't think so."

"What do you suggest then?"

"Let's wait and see," said Sammy.

"For God's sake, how long more are we going to wait?"

"For as long as it takes us to act responsibly."

"I fail to understand you, Sammy. Truly, I fail to understand."

After much wrangling, Salwa talked him into accepting the idea of murdering Jamil. That same week, on a Saturday night, Sammy brought Komba and Highway to Nadia's home, telling Jamil they were there to fix an electric generator. Sammy left the home while Komba and Highway strangled Jamil to death with a cord. His body was buried in the same shed as that of Nadia and the dog.

Salwa assumed the identity of Nadia Ahmed in order to sell off Nadia's property. With Sammy as agent, they sold Nadia's Mercedes Benz 200 car; then two of her 10-ton Toyota trucks; then a plot of land; her saving bonds; her jewelry; and finally, the house itself. Amazingly, they managed to sell the house without getting caught, even though they asked for payment in cash, and Salwa cannot produce any identification to prove she was Nadia.

In the days that followed, the four accomplices began to argue. Sammy and Salwa were angry at Komba and Highway because they stole jewelry out of Jamil's bedroom and did not split with them. Highway found out that Komba cheated him on the payment for the murder. He vowed to find Komba and kill him. Sammy was angry with Salwa. She had been selling all the expensive items and instead of giving him half the money she was giving him pittance here and there.

Sammy was afraid that Salwa would murder him. He told Augustine, "If anything happens to me you go to the police." Augustine pointed out that there was no proof that Salwa murdered Nadia. Augustine talked to Sammy into writing a four-page confession. Sammy did this in the presence of Augustine and one Charles Fanday. Charles, a driver at the Commercial Vehicle Company, was Sammy's friend and Sammy told him about the murders. Charles refused to hear any more details and he walked out during the writing of the confession.

Charles told another driver, Arthur, about the murders. Arthur called the police. Sammy and Salwa were arrested and detained. In due course, the investigation led to the arrest and detention of Komba and Highway. Incriminating evidences collected by the police strengthened the case of the state prosecutor. When the murder trial ended, the presiding judge sentenced Komba and Highway to death by hanging while Salwa and Sammy were sentenced to life imprisonment.

7

A Suitcase Full Of Dried Fish

"Please, don't go. Don't leave me alone," Zainab Sesay pleaded, holding Foday Bangura's hand to stop him from packing his suitcase.

"I'm not leaving you but I must go," he whispered, as if trying not to wake up the others in the adjoining room. His slight stoop made him look a shade shorter than his tall, slim thirty years old body. Dark in complexion, with thin lips, pointed nose, and a narrow face made him think that he was handsome. Dressed in his favourite navy-blue trousers and a brown short-sleeved shirt, he wore a friendly look.

"Take it easy, Foday," she told him, still holding on to his hand.

They were silent for a brief moment. He ignored her and stared out the window, listening to the melodic chirping sound of the weaver birds that had colonized a palm tree in the compound. It was late in August, and the Kambia Town streets looked wet and muddy. Most of its inhabitants were still in slumber.

The previous night had left Foday trying to keep warm with the help of a blanket. Every time he closed his eyes, he would see himself inside an aircraft flying to England. Strangely enough, he had never been inside one let alone flown in it.

"You're not the only unemployed graduate in town," Zainab added.

She was in her mid-twenties, short, fair in complexion, and strongly built. She looked every inch the bread-winner of her household and there was authority in her bearing. She wore a white night gown with a head-tie to match.

"I know, but let me try somewhere else," he replied.

"When the time is ripe, you'll get a job and leave Sierra Leone for England."

"Not with all the rejections from employers."

Foday grabbed his suitcase and moved to the house's front porch. For a moment, he stood transfixed, suitcase in hand, wondering if he should leave or not. He took one look at Zainab's tearful eyes and quickly bowed his head. He should leave, he reassured himself. He had made up his mind to leave two weeks ago.

A taxi cab screeched to a stop, polluting the air with exhaust fumes. Now there was little to hold him back. Not even Zainab, his fiancé for the past two years. He bid her farewell and jumped into the cab. In bewilderment, she shook her head like a swimmer with water in her ears. Zainab shuffled indoors in a daze with a stern face.

Sitting in the front seat of the taxi cab that was taking him to the lorry park, Foday's eyes were fixed on an invisible horizon. He felt as guilty as sin for abandoning his fiancé. He sensed a strong lump in his throat as a taste of bile filled his mouth. Nevertheless, he was proud for having overcome the fear of leaving the familiar for the unknown.

He knew what he wanted, he thought, and he was going to get it rather than risk failure. He was not the type of person, like Zainab, who procrastinated indefinitely due to indecisiveness. He respected her for being a hardworking petty trader and a dedicated breadwinner since they met. But now he must leave in search of greener pastures.

Foday found himself waiting at the park for the vehicle that would take him to Freetown. Meanwhile, he sat down by the stall of a petty trader keeping himself warm from a charcoal stove used by the trader. He loved the early mornings of the rainy season when it is neither hot nor cold, and the beautiful sunrise.

A couple of hours later, Foday was seating in the front cab of the Toyota truck with the driver and a short chubby-looking young woman. She may be in her mid-twenties. She wore a blue jeans and a yellow short-sleeved blouse. The driver, dressed in military fatigues, seemed to be about forty or more years old. The truck tore along in an enraged jerky pattern on the swamp land on both sides of the road which rose and fell like a broad blanket that was being accidentally shaken.

Foday took his eyes from the window and leaned back against the seat. The driver seemed to asked himself whether to start a conversation with him or not. Finally, he broke the ice.

"Are you feeling sleepy?" the driver asked Foday. "By the way my name is Dauda."

"No, I'm not. I'm just thinking of my chances of finding a job in Freetown. Call me Foday."

"You might be lucky but be prepared to be unemployed for a long time."

"I think I am. Hopefully, I'll be staying with my paternal uncle until I find a job."

The driver brought a small plastic bottle of *Diamond Rum* from his glove compartment, opened it, took a gulp, and extended it cheerfully.

"No, thanks," Foday said.

The woman who had not spoken at all since the start of the journey moved restlessly on her seat. She pouted her lower lip with contempt and said, "When you drive, don't drink".

"You're right, madam," said Dauda, wiping his lips with the back of his hand. "I'm drinking to my friend here. Good luck in your search for employment."

"Thank you, but you sound pessimistic," said Foday.

"Well, it's the way life goes in this country that baffles me. I was once a primary school teacher. I had been forced to leave the teaching job and become a driver."

"Why?"

"I left because of the delay in payment of monthly salaries."

"That's too bad. I'm a graduate with a B.A. degree in French."

"Hmm . . . French?" said Dauda, coughing slightly. "An academic degree doesn't matter much in Freetown."

"I'll see how it goes," said Foday, trying to end the discussion.

On several occasions, their journey was interrupted by traffic policemen demanding to see their particulars, or to receive bribes.

"If any institution in this country is long overdue for change, it is the police force," said a frustrated Dauda.

"They need to restore the image of the police service in order to build public confidence in it," said the woman.

"I think that the poor conditions of service of police officers unquestionably reflect the poor levels of commitment and the lack of professionalism," pointed out Foday.

"The infrastructure of the service is appalling and need to be upgraded. At the moment, the salaries of officers, particularly recruits, are so poor that they can hardly motivate new applicants," said Dauda.

The woman then added an encouraging note: "I heard that an investigation led by the Inspector-General of Police made some recommendations to the government regarding the conditions of service of officers, and it is yet to be seen whether they would be effective."

"Only a radical overhaul of the police service would bring change. An incremental overhaul would be a joke as the situation has become a cankerworm in the society," said Foday.

Waving his hand dismissively, Dauda suggested, "I think confidential telephone lines for the public to report officers who breach the integrity and professional standards set up should be launched to restore public confidence in the police service."

"That's right", said the woman, "especially if such confidential service is monitored, by independent monitors."

The lorry was now passing through a vast palm tree plantation. Foday gave a long whistle.

"Boy, it's hot in here!" he said.

"The wind might pick up later," said Dauda, and smiled at him amiably.

Foday looked out the window and straightened his shirt collar. Zainab was always doing that for him. Suddenly he felt helpless without her. He shifted his position, accidentally touched the foot of the woman.

"Sorry," Foday murmured.

"It's alright," the woman said. She pulled her skirt over her exposed legs. "Which part of Freetown would you be staying?"

"In the east end," Foday said.

"Oh. I'm residing in the east too," she said turning to take a closer look at him.

"Well, we may come across each other again," Foday smiled at her.

"I don't think I've introduced myself," she said, shaking hands with him. "Tenneh Turay."

"Foday Bangura. Glad to meet you."

Dauda, who was silently concentrating on his driving, glanced over just as they were shaking hands, and sighed.

"I live in the Fourah Bay community. Ever been there?"

Foday shook his head.

"Nice place to live." She smiled, showing healthy white teeth.

"You don't mind giving me your address?" Foday asked amusedly.

"Number 7 Taylor Street, the house opposite McCarthy Street," she replied without hesitation.

"Thank you. I'll pay you a visit. Maybe you might help me find a job."

Dauda coughed lightly, as if to say, I can hear you. There was an awkward silence when they had nothing to say to each other. Foday wondered if he should ask Tenneh some more questions. What did it matter after all? He thought.

Suddenly, he asked:

"What do you do for a living?"

"I work as a secretary for a Lebanese merchant."

"Making good money, eh?" Foday said interestedly.

"Not really. I just make the minimum to survive."

"That's better than no job at all."

"That's true," Tenneh went on. "All I need now is a matrimonial home." She laughed with real pleasure, and slapped her thigh.

"When I get a job, I'll meet you so that we can make a home," said Foday, giving Tenneh a broad smile and coquettish wink.

Her eyes were dancing as an eager joy gave vitality to her cheeks.

Once more Dauda coughed and glanced at them. He told them that they were now closer to Freetown.

Suddenly, Tenneh's eyes were downcast with a delicate coyness. Like the two men, she remained silent for the rest of the journey.

✄ ✄ ✄

Slowly, Foday walked on Kennedy Street to his uncle, Sorie Bangura's home. The tropical sun had just set and the street was fairly crowded with people going up and down. Hawkers were busy selling their wares like patched groundnuts, fruits, and kerosene for lighting lamps. Some children were playing hopscotch while others were noisily playing hide and seek. He had learnt that in Freetown you had to come to terms with noise. He was glad he did not meet anyone on the street he had to speak to as he felt tired and resigned.

"I'm doing well, uncle," he said with a smile when he met Sorie Bangura, his wife, and four children.

His uncle greeted him with an anxious lift of his arms. "I'm pleased to hear that." He pulled a chair and sat down to listen. He was a small man with grey hair, a handsome face at age seventy. Foday knew Sorie to be a cheerful person, who unlike him, hardly nursed his grievances.

"Make yourself at home, and you'll be sharing a room with your cousin, Amadu," Sorie said delightfully.

On Monday of the following week, Foday started his job search. He was accompanied by his teenage cousin, Amadu, who looked very much like his father, Sorie. Armed with his curriculum vitae and copies of his certificates, he went to one of the government departments at New England Ville. The manager he approached spoke Mende to him instead of English, the official language. Foday did not understand Mende which was the language of the ruling political party. As he could not respond, the manager laughed at him and told him in Krio that there was no job vacancy. When they went out of the office, Amadu said, irritably:

"This is one reason why I didn't go to college. You complete your studies and you find no job."

"But that shouldn't stop you from going to college," said Foday.

"Okay, I'm a loafer, so what?" he shrugged with a twisting movement of his narrow shoulders.

"Who said you were?"

"My father says so. He should've had a good son like you."

"What makes you think I'm good?"

"I mean you take your studies seriously, and now you're looking for work. I don't feel like working. I don't have to work. The country has been destroyed by tribalism and corruption. So is there any reason I should work if I don't have to?"

Foday looked at him sadly and shook his head. If only his cousin will be more resilient, he thought. But was he himself resilient? He wondered. He swallowed his grief and anger and disappointment at the way the manager had treated him. They returned home to a cheerful Sorie who counseled him not to worry. "You'll get a job at the right time."

There was so much to look forward to now. His quest for employment was still number one on his list of priorities, his goal to immigrate to England, and then Zainab. He would propose marriage to Zainab once he was ready to leave the country.

Overhead, the sky was a clear strong blue on the day Foday visited Tenneh. The sun rays cascaded glowingly, not gold-coloured but blanched, like an object grown white with its own heat. Tenneh sat down with him on the verandah. His heart could not stop racing anytime he glanced at her. She spoke in a relaxed manner:

"Nice weather." She smiled and quickly pulled down her brightly flowered chiffon dress over her legs. He reminded himself that half a man's troubles were caused by women. But this particular woman looked friendly, he thought. He was served a glass of ginger beer and some biscuits.

"How are you, Tenneh?" Involuntarily he glanced at her short and chubby figure.

"I'm fine, thanks. Have you found yourself a job?"

"Not yet, but I'm hopeful," he said smiling.

"Listen, I would like you to meet a man at the national airlines who is looking for a tutor to teach French to his son."

"Is that right?" He asked joyfully.

"That's right, my friend, go and see him tomorrow."

"I'll definitely do so. Thank you very much," he said with a wistful admiring smile.

Before they parted company, they reminisced about their trip from Kambia to Freetown; made jokes about Dauda the driver who drove and drank alcohol.

✘ ✘ ✘

That evening, Foday Bangura was lying in bed trying to read a novel entitled *I Would Rather Stay Poor* by James Hadley Chase. The light from a kerosene lamp in the room was flickering, thereby hurting his eyes. As he was restless to go to sleep, he went outdoors for some fresh air. He did not think much of the neighbourhood. Apart from the fluctuating electricity and water supplies, it was noisy. Few hours later, after tossing and turning in bed, he managed to fall asleep in the sweltering heat.

Before eight o'clock the next day, Foday was waiting in the female secretary's office of the man at the airlines. When he learnt from her that the man was the Financial Controller of the airlines, he became more anxious to meet him. Afraid of the unknown, eager to acquire a job, he felt sweat dripping from his armpit.

He knew how fear can stifle one's thinking and actions. It can create indecisiveness resulting in stagnation. He knew of talented people who procrastinated indefinitely rather than risk failure. He was not going to lose this opportunity or erode his confidence. No downward spiral, he assured himself.

The man breezed into the office by half past eight. He was of average height, dark in complexion, and appeared to be in his late forties. He wore a grey-coloured suit and a red tie. In less than fifteen minutes of his arrival, he invited Foday to join him in his office.

"Hello, my name is Bull, John Bull," said the man, shaking Foday's hand.

"Good morning, sir. Foday Bangura is my name. I'm pleased to meet you."

"You're welcome. Take the sir off. Please have a seat."

"Thank you."

"So you speak and write French?"

"Yes, I do."

"I would like you to teach French to my son."

"When would you like me to start?"

John Bull reached into one of his top drawers and brought out a French text book and said:

"Can you read this paragraph for me?"

Foday read the paragraph eloquently. John looked at him like a hero-worshiping little boy and beamed, "Excellent, you can start the day after tomorrow."

"You mean I can start that soon?"

"Sure, let me give you my address. I hope that you'll be available to teach three days a week."

"Yes, I will be available."

✼ ✼ ✼

Three months later, John Bull presented Foday with two employment options within the national airlines. He was asked to choose between the job of an accounts clerk and that of an air steward. After consultation with Tenneh who had now become his girlfriend, he chose to become an air steward. He believed that the flying position will be a stepping stone to achieve his goal of immigrating to England.

In one of the classroom sessions during his two weeks training to become an air steward, Foday remembered asking the female Jordanian tutor: "Why does an aircraft fly?"

"Aerodynamics," she said. "An aircraft flies because of the flow of air on the curvature of its wing. The faster a gas moves, the lower its pressure. As air moves faster across the top of the wing, it creates a vacuum which brings the wing upwards, thereby lifting the aircraft."

Foday was flabbergasted by the amount of knowledge he acquired about the precision of the Boeing 707 aircraft design. Especially, the way parts were shaped to within a hundredth of an inch.

Foday's first flight on duty as an air steward took him on a same-day round trip to Monrovia, Abidjan, and Lagos. Being his first time to ever fly in an aircraft, he was so anxious that he forgot to wear his uniform name badge. During the flight, the purser asked permission from the Turkish captain for him to visit the cockpit. The first officer, a handsome fellow from Tanzania, briefly described their surroundings.

"Out here in the front is the control panel consisting of three video screens: flight display, navigation display, and systems display."

Pointing upwards, he said, "That's the overhead instrument panel. And the pedestal is this box-shaped structure between my seat and that of the captain." The captain turned his head and gave Foday a nod and a smile.

The first officer tapped the pedestal and explained, "Here we've levers that operate the flaps, throttles, spoilers, brakes, and thrusters. Directly behind me is our flight engineer, who among other duties monitors the performance of the four engines."

During de-briefing at the end of the flight, Foday learnt that they had to fly the last leg of the trip without functional radar. This meant that the pilots had to fly the aircraft by visual means and by VHF radio. Fortunately for them though it was a day flight and the weather was in their favour.

By the time Foday completed his ninety days work probationary period, he had been to Las Palmas, Paris, and London on several occasions. At the same time, he was renting a one-bedroom apartment house in the Brookfields area of Freetown. Tenneh wanted to live with him but he asked her to wait for the appropriate time. Tenneh had started talking about engagement and marriage. For a long time, she had been frustrated in her hunger for a husband. And he seemed to be a God-sent suitor.

Frequently, she will utter phrases like: "Our engagement and marriage will be a talk of the town." "My love for you is as deep as the ocean." "My love is like a red, red rose." Although she would try to sound romantic, yet her words would come out in that distant, expressionless tone that terrified him. Most of the time, he would say less or avoid the subject, claiming to be tired. Worst of all she would continue to nag him. Then the dreaminess in her brown eyes would disperse for a while like a mist. There was inside him, like a defect in a jewel, a fear and apprehension of trouble with the issue of Tenneh and Zainab.

Even though they were miles apart, Zainab was still looking forward to him as a fiancé. She always thought that there was not much of a gulf that separated her life from his. She expected Foday to go to England where she would join him in marriage and raise children.

He thought of England with a shiver of uncertainty. Whenever he was overwhelmed by this thought, something would throb in his chest, like the breaking of his heart. He would then ponder if the precarious life he was willing to lead overseas, for the sake of himself and Zainab, was of greater worth as compared to his present life. Moreover, England would be too dismal a prospect without Zainab. And what will become of Tenneh? Oh well, for now, he was even scared to think about that.

Although he had been unemployed for a considerable period of time, his life up to now had not been that pathless, and seeking had seen some sense of direction. At least his university studies had revealed a meaning. He now has a job. He had never imagined he would work for an airline company, but to his surprise he had found that his practicality was suited to the industry's culture.

✄ ✄ ✄

In less than two years, while still on the job as air steward, Foday became interested in the politics of the Association of Travel and Hospitality Workers. Soon, his excellent interpersonal relation with his peers earned him the post of president of the association. This was a position of considerable visibility. Its members were often unhappy with decisions they themselves had made, blaming him if employers had not improved their conditions of service, or if there was in-fighting within the association. It took composure and diplomacy to keep everybody happy and get problems resolved. Foday, a born conciliator, was especially good at this.

In return for walking a diplomatic tightrope, he had the run of the association. As president, Foday was involved in every aspect of the association's work; he had a lot of freedom and absolute responsibility. The *Daily Mail* had printed a column about him and the association; it was quite impressive in a newspaper. It had made him feel important. The realization of his importance dazzled his mind. But this did not go without challenges within the association, ranging from insults to threats.

Once upon a time, he had a heated argument with an opposing member of the association which led him to consider resignation
from the post. Salia Bockarie, the opposing member, was a ticketing
and reservation officer at Yazbeck Travel Agency. Salia was a ruthless
and periodically reckless man. He was short and heavily-built; his
chin thrust forward, ready to fight. In a way, he looked like a black
mamba ready to strike. Infamously coarse and vulgar, he was quick to
lose his temper. During that association's meeting that almost led to
his resignation, Foday said:

"I would like to point out that we're not here to make blind arguments and be boisterous. Unproven accusations are inhuman and
only perpetuate ignorance among those who believe that they could
act as bulldogs."

With open animosity, a couple of members shuffled out of the
meeting. Foday caught the hard look on Salia's unsmiling face. He
ignored him and continued:

"Let's don't forget that this is a voluntary organization and there
are no stipends paid to the executive. Foday's eyes with their keen and
inquiring look gave him away as someone who was spoiling for a fight.
And in response, Salia spat out his words venomously:

"Mr Bangura, I am utterly disappointed at you. If this is the leg-
acy you want to bestow to your descendants, then you are a joker. If
a wise man doesn't respect himself, then he would be considered an
imbecile. Your common sense has become ambiguous. If your reasoning is so irreparable, then you shouldn't be the president of this
association."

The silence that followed was a blood-curdling one. Heads rolled
from side to side. Foday glanced about for air. The room had become
a little hell. He wanted to shout back, but instead his voice out came
like a whisper: "Shut up."

"Did I hear you say shut up?" Salia inquired, punctuating it with
an undisguised leer. Foday kept quiet. His eyes were getting red with
anger. His temples were pounding.

With an unwavering gaze, Salia kept talking.

"See how low you can go. I'm not insulting you but telling you the truth without exaggeration. So don't tell me to shut up. I feel sorrow for your descendants if they are to have your kind of attitude."

The meeting ended without the normal decorum. Foday likened Salia as the type of creature that slithered into town quietly so no one would notice when he dug his fangs in and slowly poisoned their minds.

Foday felt tired and lonely when he went to his one-bedroom apartment house that night. His cell phone rang. He picked it up.

"Hello . . ."

"Shut your trap, idiot," a voice said. "You want problem, you'll get it. We're watching you."

Click

He stood in his bedroom, holding the phone in his hand. Infrequently, he was never one to brood when things went askew, but he had a horrible sinking feeling. He moved to the window and looked out at the empty dimly-lit street. He saw three men standing a short distance from his apartment.

Hell.

He went to the main door, bolted it. All over his body, little muscles twitched and quivered. Then he turned off the bedroom lights, pressed his body to the wall, and peeped out the window.

The men were still standing there. They were talking now. As he watched, one of them pointed toward his apartment.

He reached underneath his bed, found a club.

Again he peeped out the window.

And the men were walking toward his apartment.

They were casually dressed, in Tee-shirts and jeans, but they looked cruel and tough as nails. As they moved forward they split up, one walking to the window, the other walking toward the door. Foday felt as if he was in a world of silence and total blackness. He saw the trap he was in. Gripping the club, he moved around the bedroom. Peeping through the window, he saw one of them standing there ram-rod straight. The third man was looking up and down the street guardedly.

He heard the sound of soft footsteps, coming closer to the door. He thought about Zainab, and then Tenneh. He wondered how they will receive the news if he was killed by these men. What do they want from him? Is Salia Bockarie involved in this plot?

He crouched down, fumbled with the club. He tried to stand up but his legs were rubber. He realized he could not hear the footsteps anymore. Gingerly, he raised his head until he could peep out of the bottom corner of the window.

The man was heading back to the street. Then he heard a faint sound, like a knock on the door. He felt panic. He waited, perspiring profusely.

"You," said a voice from the door that sounded like that of a wolf.

Foday heard footsteps retreating from the door. He ran to the window and saw the three men walking away into the darkness. He leaned on the wall looking so transparently silly and pitiable.

Get some sleep, he told himself. But he could not sleep. Every time he closed his eyes, he could see the three men standing on the street. He had a gut feeling that those men were related to his activities as president of the association. Foday thought that resignation from the presidency should be the solution. And maybe it was high time he intensified his drive toward his goal of immigrating to England.

⚹ ⚹ ⚹

Like the aggressive thrust of an aircraft, Foday quickly submitted a visitor's visa application to the British High Commission in Freetown. After the interview, the male visa officer said:

"You have not satisfied me that you would leave England at the end of your stay. There are a number of inconsistencies and contradictions in your application."

Foday was so upset that he protested, "Sir, I tried to call the visa office on several occasions to clarify certain points but nobody answered to the telephone."

"I'm sorry but our decision is final," the visa officer said dismissively.

Foday left the interview wondering why his application was denied by an office that did not answer to telephone calls; an office that one can neither email nor write a letter.

"It's sad — it's really sad," he said to himself.

A couple of weeks later while conversing with an immigration lawyer, the strikingly beautiful Sierra Leonean – Gambian lady said:

"I am sorry to hear you were refused the visa. But, perhaps, you can re-apply."

"Yes, I'll do so," Foday responded emphatically.

"The main criterion for offering you a visa would be whether it appears to the immigration authorities that you would return to Sierra Leone at the end of your visit," the lawyer said.

"But I planned to return," he lied.

"Did you have an invitation letter from a friend or relative in England?"

"No, I had none," he said, thinking back.

"No doubt such a letter could have been of some assistance to you. If you know someone who would be willing to write and invite you, it may increase your chances."

Foday's lip curled in disgust for not having thought of getting such a letter.

"How is the letter written?" he asked.

"Your friend or relative should indicate that they will be responsible for your accommodation while you are visiting England. They should indicate the dates you are being invited and when you will leave."

Foday wanted to ask another question but the lady, looking as cool as a cucumber, kept talking. She seemed to be a person whose strength and dignity were her clothing.

"The letter must also indicate your name, date of birth, address and telephone number, his or her relationship to you and the purpose of your trip. Your friend or relative must also state their name, date of birth, address, telephone number and occupation. They must indicate their status in England as a permanent resident or citizen and include a photocopy of a document proving that status."

As she advised Foday, her cool and calm nature was as refreshing to him as an ice pack.

"Sometimes I . . ." He wanted to ask but pride kept him from asking. He felt somehow ashamed. The lawyer continued speaking:

"Perhaps visiting in the summer may be a better time to start. There are many attractions in summer. It would be good for you to be specific about which attractions you would like to see. It appears you may have been vague in your application. Try to give much detail about why you would like to visit England."

It was slowly dawning on Foday that he had not taken the right steps in his previous visa application. Now, he was looking more convinced that his next visa application would pass the test of time. He felt joyful. With the amount of information the lawyer had given him, he thought the cat was now out of the bag.

It appeared as if the lawyer had something more to say. As there would be no one as knowledgeable to speak to when the problems assailed him, he continued to listen.

"It is good that you have had steady employment and some money in the bank, as you must show that you will return to Sierra Leone at the end of your visit, as well as sufficient funds to maintain yourself while on your visit. You could also provide a letter from your employer, indicating the length of your employment with them and when they expect you back at work. Obviously, you need to have a valid passport."

Tersely, Foday inquired, "what if I'm denied the visa again?"

A frown creased her face, and she responded:

"If you are turned down again, your host could, under certain circumstances, seek judicial review of the decision from a court in England. However, in order to do this, you would need to seek legal assistance from a lawyer out there."

A tide of satisfaction ran through Foday like ripples from a stone cast in water. He felt as happy as a clam. For him, the lawyer's advice had appeared as a light in a sea of darkness.

❃ ❃ ❃

Foday waited for three months before re-submitting another visitor's visa application form to the British High Commission. During the interview, the female visa officer turned to him with the faintest smile of self-consciousness on her lips because he had been staring at her. He saw that her smile stayed, tinged with perplexity, perhaps annoyance. She made a movement as if she would wipe him away like a chalk streak on a blackboard. He clenched his hand as cold sweat appeared on his forehead.

"Mr. Bangura, can you please go and wait at the reception," she said.

After a brief wait, his name was called and his passport handed over to him with a three-month visa. He almost screamed and jumped with joy. Once out of the High Commission, he ran like the wind.

When he called Zainab over the telephone to inform her, she said:

"Life is amazing, you never know what you're going to get. Foday, my dear, you're the sun in my sky."

He then told Tenneh. She cried out with joy, kissing him all over his face.

"Wow! But that is as easy as shooting fish in a barrel," she said.

"It wasn't that easy as you think," he said.

Within three weeks, Foday made the necessary preparations for his trip to London via Paris. His supervisor at the airlines approved his entitlement to a two-week leave with pay, plus a free return air ticket and one day transit in Paris. Tenneh packed him a suitcase full of dried fish for sale in London. He bade farewell to Zainab, his uncle Sorie and cousin Amadu.

It was a long night flight and Foday breathed out heavily as the trip was coming to an end. He was expecting to arrive in Paris within one hour. Intermittent sleep was all he got during the rough flight.

He yawned and rubbed his eyes as the morning sunlight penetrated through the window of the aircraft.

Momentarily, he heard an announcement over the speakers asking passengers and cabin crew to return to their seats. Cecilia, a friendly colleague of Foday, was rushing along the aisle towards the first-class cabin. The seat belt signs came on and within a few minutes, the aircraft seemed to shudder. It felt like it was nose-diving. Foday saw Cecilia being thrown around. Some lockers opened and luggage fell out. Suddenly he was lifted off his seat. He felt light and sick to his stomach. A baby cried while a couple of passengers screamed. Others cursed. What a turbulence and a challenge to achieving his goal, he thought, and recited a prayer.

The pilot aborted the landing and the aircraft was diverted to Nice, in southern France, where it landed safely and routinely. With the exception of Cecilia, who was taken to hospital with a suspected broken hip, all passengers and crew were transported to Paris by an iDBUS coach.

By the time the coach arrived in Paris, Foday's suitcase full of dried fish was completely infested with maggots. He cursed the bad weather that brought about the flight diversion. Helplessly, he swallowed his disappointment before dumping the suitcase and its rotten contents into the hotel's garbage bin.

The next day, looking as bright as a button, Foday boarded a SNCF train that would take him from Paris to the Calais Ferry Port, in northern France. From there, he planned to cross the English Channel to London.

Half way through the train journey, he was intercepted by the immigration officer on board the train. He instructed Foday to discontinue his journey and return to Paris.

"But why shouldn't I continue?"

"You don't have a visa for France," said the officer with a typical French nasal accent.

"I'm an air steward and we don't normally have a visa."

"That's why you should stay within the airport surroundings."

Dumbfounded, Foday was now at the mercy of the dismissive-looking officer.

"We'll disembark in Amiens, and I'll see you off the train to Paris"

In a couple of hours later, Foday found himself at the Hilton Paris Orly airport hotel. In situations like this, he remembered Zainab used to say, you had better pull your socks up. Disappointed but yet courageous, he frantically made air travel arrangement for the next day. At the Charles De Gaulle airport, fully-dressed in his air steward uniform, he was allowed to board a British Airways aircraft by an immigration officer. He was feeling elated when he finally arrived in London.

8

The Nairobi School Girl

She stood transfixed by the closed classroom door. Her pencil skirt highlighted a protruding hip line while her brown fingers clasped a pile of books.

It was not a usual sight at the Alliance-Ravals Girls' High School at a time when the Nairobi-based boarding home was closed for vacation. In the last sixty-six years or so, many a schoolgirl had walked in the light of the school but none that Juma Otieno could remember had stood unattended on an empty corridor, early on a Friday morning. But then again, apart from his Physics laboratory end-of-term check visit, he had been gone from the compound for two months and things might have changed.

He glanced up and down the recognizable corridor with the same classroom doors that he had known for the past five years. Nothing had changed though. The recognition both bothered and appeased him. He looked again, gaping, attempting to find other pupils.

Not a single one.

In his mid-forties, he was no longer used to eccentricities after a two month stint in his home town of Nyakach where a school girl unattended on a school corridor during vacation would be a surprise. But in Nairobi it was usual. The school girl stood still like a deity.

As he was totally charmed, his intense desire to know her heightened. That was where he ought to have ended it. But he did not. Aware that a further probe on the school girl will consume his time to check the laboratory and join his wife Akeyo for lunch, he nevertheless decided to investigate. He knew that once brought into the fold of Akeyo, he will not be leaving home for the rest of the day.

Although his dream was to do so, Juma Otieno, unlike some male teachers in the school, had never pursued a discreet relationship with any female student.

He moved closer to the school girl in a couple of quick strides, with the heat of the air permeating his heavy woollen coat. He kicked himself mentally for not having dressed casually. The school girl in her pencil skirt made him stand out like a sore thumb.

The school girl had her side to him and as he got closer he noticed how the skirt fitted her like a glove. On hearing his footsteps, she turned, the pile of books swaying severely in her grasp.

He beamed, concluding she looked like an aggressively enterprising Kikuyu. The V-shaped neckline of her Tee-shirt sat on full breasts and a gold necklace adorned a lanky neck which moved into a sharp chin. Her long braids dropped onto her prominent forehead, and tiny pimples extended across a pointed nose that some might call pretty.

"You seem to have missed the library." He stretched out his arm showing the way. "It's next to the assembly hall."

Juma Otieno was at home with bug-eyed responses from school girls, usually followed by a flirtatious sly smile. He knew this was to do with his Luo ancestry. Time and again, he wished he did not have the usual black hair and brown eyes but he would not exchange his height for whatever. Nevertheless this schoolgirl's glowing gaze hit him like a ton of bricks. "I know. I'm a pupil in this school. Aren't you the Physics teacher?"

"Ah! So you're no stranger."

"Thanks for the direction anyway," she said, looking doubtful of what next to do or say.

"What's your name?"

"My name's Mwara."

"Mwara, hmmm . . . Call me Juma."

"Mr. Otieno," she said.

"Juma," he insisted, "Do you live in this area?"

"Yes, across the road. I live with my mother, Mumbi."

"I live in the adjoining neighbourhood next to yours. Can I invite you for some snacks at my friend's house?"

She hesitated briefly and gave him a positive nod.

His heart skipped a beat as his eyes caressed her voluptuous figure. They made an appointment for the next day. He gave her the address of his friend, Jaramogi.

✖ ✖ ✖

On that fateful Saturday evening in February 2010, teacher Juma Otieno anxiously wanted to meet sixteen years old Mwara, the Nairobi school girl. Akeyo, his wife, did not want him to leave their two-bedroom rented apartment.

"Where are you going Juma?" Akeyo inquired in an unpleasant tone. She was to him a beauty, the angelic face, soulful brown eyes, the delicately fragile but perfectly formed body.

"I need to see Jaramogi," he said, while thinking about the younger and even more charming Akeyo.

"I've an urgent matter to discuss with you," as if intending to blame him for something.

"We'll talk about that when I'm back," he said dismissively as though her issue really did not matter.

"Juma! It's about my visit to the hospital," cried Akeyo. Her chest was heavy with repressed sobs.

He bolted out of the house, jumped into his aging two-door sedan Toyota Celica car and drove away.

Half way through the journey, his car broke down. He left the vehicle at a roadside garage and decided to board a *Matatu* commercial van. It was then he realized that he had forgotten his wallet at home. He stood on the sidewalk, perplexed as a lump of anger rose in his throat.

A beige-coloured Nissan Pathfinder stopped in front of him, its horn blaring. He peeped into the cab only to see the handsome-looking young man, Paul Kimani, the handsome young Geography teacher at the school.

At age thirty-two, Paul was always elegantly dressed, always wearing the sweet smell of Serge Lutens' Borneo 1834 Cologne for men. At the Alliance-Ravals Girls' High School, some referred to him as 'the show man', others considered him as a womanizer. He believed that when it came to women being attracted to him, his smell was what will get them hooked.

"Come in, my friend. You must be looking for a ride," said Paul, smiling cheerfully.

"My goodness! You came along at the right time," said Juma Otieno, as he jumped into Kimani's four-wheel drive.

"You must be heading to see your sweetheart," said Kimani.

"No. I'm going to see a relative of mine; about ten minutes by car from here."

"Don't worry, my friend. It's Saturday," said Kimani, patting Juma Otieno on his lap.

Rumours had been going around that Paul Kimani was having a discreet relationship with one of the girls in the school. Juma Otieno secretly admired him, and wished he too could have a relationship with any of the most beautiful students.

Within five minutes, Paul Kimani and Juma Otieno got stuck in a traffic jam. Juma Otieno took a glance at his wristwatch and drew in sharp angry breaths. He was already late to meet Mwara.

"What's the matter, my friend?" inquired Paul Kimani.

"Let me come down and walk the remaining distance," said Juma Otieno.

"Come on, my friend; let's be chatting while the traffic jam clears up."

"Thanks, but I'm running late," said Juma Otieno, as he alighted from the vehicle.

He waved Paul Kimani goodbye and practically ran to his destination. He was just in time to see Mwara leaving, accompanied by Jaramogi. Juma Otieno convinced her to stay for a while. Jaramogi gave him the key to his one-bedroom apartment and left for an evening stroll.

Mwara wore a navy-blue miniskirt with a rainbow-coloured blouse; her ear-rings — small golden studs — sat tightly on her earlobes. Her long braids tied into a ponytail. She glanced uneasily at him.

"Relax, my dear. You look so lovely," he said.

She thawed under his compliments. As she smiled at Juma Otieno, her rainbow-coloured blouse seemed to smile too. Did she know he had an eye on her? He wondered, as she sat crossed-legged on a sofa. She stared at him in rapt admiration at his handsome looks.

Striding briskly to the refrigerator, he grabbed two bottles of Fanta soda and placed them on a stool beside her. He reached out to the table for a box of cream crackers which he opened and offered to her. He turned on the radio and tuned in to Kiss 100 FM, Kenya's Number 1 hit music station. Donna Summer's song, *Bad Girls*, filled the air.

"Music is good for the soul," he remarked, thinking that his daydreams were verging on reality.

Mwara nodded in agreement and asked him:

"Are you married?"

"I'm separated," he replied licking his lips.

"Why didn't you invite me to your house?"

"It's a long story. You'll know with time," he promised her.

Juma Otieno could not wait any longer. He started to caress Mwara. His vision was clouding over with lust.

"I'm a virgin," she said as every part of her body called out to be touched and savoured. Her eyes glinted.

"I see. Then gently does it," he reassured her, and continued his exploits.

"No! Stop it!" She cried, as her heart fluttered with fear. The spark died out of her eyes.

Teacher Juma Otieno could not resist his feelings. He forced himself on his school girl. On the sofa, to the sound of music, he made love to Mwara who fought him like a tigress.

In less than five minutes, he had sown the seed of disruption. His shirt was sodden and clogged against his back. He could feel the sweat dripping from his armpits. He put on a penitent smile, and both of them felt as if they had just finished triathlons in a row. Strangely though, Mwara found the act pleasurable though painful at certain moments. She tried to check her sobs and began to dress up.

"All should be fine. Just don't tell anybody about it," said Juma Otieno, tapping her familiarly on her shoulder.

"Leave me alone!" She said, feeling like an idiot.

Juma Otieno promised to give her some money later, and both of them left the house, shuffling homewards in different directions. She walked on in a daze.

By the time he was home to face Akeyo, he had regained his composure, though he felt remorseful for his act with Mwara. By no stretch of the imagination could he be described as leading an exemplary life as a teacher, he thought. Neither had he demonstrated any of the school's core values.

Akeyo wasted no time in telling him about the result of her visit to the hospital.

"I've been diagnosed with meningitis," she said pathetically.

"Oh, my God," he gasped. "I'm sorry to hear that, Akeyo."

"Why should this happen to me, Juma?"

"Don't worry, my dear, you'll get better," he said with apprehension, knowing fully well that his family health care insurance coverage at the school needed to be renewed.

She noted a flicker of doubt in his eyes, and gazed around inquiringly thinking that Juma's love for her may not stand the test of her illness. All she could do now was to hang on for dear life, she thought.

Juma could not believe his eyes at the sudden change in Akeyo's appearance. Her beauty had now become a deception. Would she still be as supple and graceful as she used to be? He wondered.

⚹ ⚹ ⚹

Several weeks later, Mwara was in an early morning deep sleep, fully clothed, when Mumbi, her mother walked into her bedroom. She gave her a couple of pats on her shoulder. "Wake up, Mwara. It's time for school," she called.

She woke up sluggishly, looking worn out. Sitting up on the bed, she rubbed her eyes and yawned.

"Are you alright?" Mumbi asked.

Mwara just shrugged.

"Is something the matter?"

She shook her head and began to hiccup.

At age forty-one, Mumbi of average height was almost a replica of her daughter: full breasts, lanky neck, sharp chin, and that angelic beauty. Her hair, always plaited prettily down her narrow nape, was as black as an Egyptian night. She loved to grease it every weekend. The sweet smell of that grease, called *Dax*, always made Mwara feel sleepy.

Mumbi sat down on the bed, drew Mwara to her. In her arms she began to sob badly.

"Tell me what's wrong," she said, trying to comfort her.

As if in response to her mother, Mwara grabbed the bed sheet and vomited onto it. She felt breathless, like someone having a hangover, a mild headache. She was sweating excessively, feeling too hot. She made an attempt to stand up but her knees were weak. Panic-stricken, Mumbi guided Mwara to the bathroom where an attempt to brush her teeth brought more vomit. Even the smell of an opened bottle of Mwara's favourite shower gel made her tummy go wild.

"I hope it's not what I'm suspecting," said Mumbi.

"Mama, I'm sick," said Mwara.

"Dress up and let's go see Dr. King'angi."

Meanwhile, as a First Aid treatment, Mumbi gave her daughter some biscuits to stop the vomit. She asked her to nibble on them whenever she felt like she was going to be sick.

Dr. King'angi was a cheerful man in his fifties. Sturdy of bone, heavy of feature, many considered him as the most well-known gynecologist in the country. Others saw him as the devilish King of abortion. He preferred speaking Swahili rather than English. Dr. King'angi was always fuming over British colonization of Kenya. He thought the *Mau Mau* society did a great job in helping to get rid of the colonialists. Dr. King'angi wasted no time in performing a human chorionic gonadotropin (HCG) pregnancy test on Mwara. The result showed positive.

"Lord, have mercy!" Mumbi cried out, placing her arms on her head. She jumped around the consulting room wailing and stamping her feet on the floor as tears ran down her cheek.

Once she regained her composure, Mumbi said to Dr. King'angi, "Doctor, this pregnancy must be aborted!"

The doctor gave her a stern look and said, "Go and think about it and give me a call later."

Mumbi started to protest but Dr. King'angi dismissed her.

When they returned home, Mumbi breathed fire and brimstone on Mwara. She asked her daughter to spill the beans.

"Who's the two-left-footed monster that did this to you?"

The words were lost on Mwara's ears. She stood absent-minded unable to reply until Mumbi shouted at her.

"Mwara!

"Yes, mama," she said, trembling like someone with high fever.

Her mother's usual concern for her progress, comfort and safety sometimes irritated her. But with this incident, Mumbi's concern was in place, she thought.

"I'm asking you. Who's he?"

Without any further hesitation, she replied, "Mr. Otieno."

"Who? An uncircumcised Mr. Otieno?"

"He's my school teacher."

"He's your what?"

Averting her face, Mwara took couple of strides towards Mumbi and embraced her. "Please forgive me, Mama," she said sobbing.

Mother and daughter embraced each other and wept. They wept and wept until their eyes were swollen like a river about to burst its banks.

Mumbi looked at Mwara closely. Her eyes glinted resentfully and said:

"Do you realize that you're an Alliance-Ravals Girls' High School student and not one from those riff-raff schools?"

Mwara nodded speechlessly.

"Do you know how much money I spend on your schooling as a single mother?"

"Mama, I do."

"Mwara, my only child, what a financial muddle you've become!"

"Mama, please, Mama," was all she could say.

"Are we living in the Mathare or Majengo slum?"

"No, Mama, we're not."

"Am I not feeding and clothing you?"

"Yes, Mama, you're."

"Do you want to become a prostitute along K Street?"

"No, Mama, I don't want to."

"Tell me. What's the motto of your school?"

Mwara hesitated briefly and said in a trembling voice, as if reading from a book:

"Mama, it's to become a leading and most favoured High School . . . in the provision of quality, and, and . . . excellent education for . . ."

"Mwara, you and Otieno are not fit to be in that school. You're a disgrace, a shame," Mumbi said in tears. No matter how acidic her tongue, Mwara knew that her mother would be able to handle the situation. She respected her as a hard-working civil servant whose husband died prematurely in a road accident.

Juma Otieno's relationship with Mwara has created a rift between mother and daughter. Mumbi had a sick feeling that the pregnancy may not be aborted. So, unable to contain her frustration any longer, Mwara's distraught mother approached the school authorities to report Juma Otieno's sordid sexual relationship with her daughter.

"We no longer enjoy the good relationship that I used to have with my daughter," she told Mrs. Tina Njuguna, the school's principal.

Juma Otieno was summoned by Mrs. Njuguna. He decided not to appear as he was informed by Paul Kimani that the police will be there to arrest him. Meanwhile, Mwara was expelled instantly from the school. There had been a time when her friends would have been excited by her presence but now they were afraid to get closer to her. The news about Juma Otieno and the school girl spread like wild fire among teachers and students. The *Daily Nation* published it with the headline: *High School Teacher Defiles Female Student.*

At home, Juma Otieno explained to Akeyo the need for him to travel once again to his home town of Nyakach. "I must go and arrange with my younger sister, Abuya, for the sale of a plot of land," he said – "We need the money to offset your medical bills."

"I don't think Abuya will cooperate with you," said Akeyo.

"Why shouldn't she? After all, our late father bequeathed the plot of land to both of us."

She was silent; still looking unconvinced.

Perhaps Akeyo was right, Juma Otieno told himself. Abuya was the black sheep in the family of only two children: herself and him. Their mother passed away when both of them were less than seven years old. They had been raised by their father who had less control over Abuya. Juma Otieno vowed to convince his sister to sell the plot of land while he was in hiding. He instructed Akeyo not to tell anybody about his whereabouts.

Once he had made up his mind to leave for the town of Nyakach, Juma Otieno could not be held back by Akeyo. She had no idea that her husband was a wanted man running away from the police for having committed an inglorious act.

✖ ✖ ✖

Meanwhile, for fear of a possible loss of her life, Mwara became uncooperative with Mumbi's grand plan to terminate an unwanted pregnancy. As she refused to see Dr. King'angi, Mumbi started giving her a concoction of herbs. Mwara's health deteriorated to almost the point of death. For a couple of days, she was admitted at the Aga Khan University Hospital in Nairobi. Once discharged, Mumbi decided to keep her daughter's pregnancy rather than risk losing her.

By the time Mwara recovered, she could hardly recollect half of what transpired during her illness. The period seemed to have passed in a flash. On the advice of Mumbi, Mwara stayed out of sight from friends and relatives as her mother planned to relocate her to the town of Thogoto, near Kikuyu in Kiambu County. This was the place where Mumbi's aging mother, Nancy Nyambura, resided in a brick house.

The house was completely built in April 1957 by Kamotho, Nyambura's husband. He was an anti-colonial activist who considered Christianity and Islam as foreign domination that struck out of nowhere like a bolt of lightning to suppress the African's way of life. He detested the idea of Kenya being a protectorate of the British Empire. Kamotho went to every nook and cranny of the country preaching against British colonialism, Christianity, and Islam. Some credited him as a key player in the 1951–1954 *Mau Mau* society's uprising. His influence on the Kikuyu people was so great that he even won activists among those who reeked of cow dung and alcohol.

A few months before Kenya gained independence in December 1963, Kamotho was imprisoned and later murdered by the British. They stripped him naked in front of other detainees, and forced him to dig his own grave, after which he was buried alive face downwards.

Kamotho's compound, now Nyambura's, was at the beginning of a straight dirt road. It's a small brick house painted black, red, and green, reflecting the colours of Kenya's national flag, and a corrugated-iron sheet roof. Its outer limit was marked by well-kept plants of Hibiscus and Yellow Bell flowers.

Dressed in a brightly-coloured *kanga*, Nyambura emerged from the shade of the house into the setting sunlight. Even though she looked like a woman in her fifties at age seventy, that grace and beauty she once had were no longer to be seen. As she wobbled like a duck to meet and greet Mwara and Mumbi, one could hardly believe that fifty years ago, she won a beauty contest. For a moment she did not recognize Mwara, who was fourteen when they last visited her. She held her arms wide, embracing Mwara, and then Mumbi.

"Come on in," Nyambura said cheerfully, leading them into the house.

"How is Jamba?" Mumbi asked of her younger sister.

"She went to the market," replied Nyambura. "Let's hope to see her soon," she sighed mournfully.

"Don't tell me she hasn't improved her behaviour," said Mumbi.

Nyambura shook her head in silence as she showed them their bedroom.

As far as Mumbi could remember, she had been responsible for the upkeep of Nyambura and Jamba. Her younger sister, Jamba, quit secondary school when she had an unwanted pregnancy for which no man claimed responsibility. Jamba gave birth to a baby boy that passed away when he was only ten months old.

For supper, Nyambura served Mumbi and Mwara the potato and corn-based *mokimo* along with chicken stew, pumpkin leaves, and tea. Once they finished eating, Mumbi took Nyambura aside and told her about the purpose of their visit: namely, Mwara's pregnancy and the need for her to stay with her grandmother.

"Aieee! *Ngai!* God help us!" Nyambura cried out, placing her arms on her head as tears ran down her cheek.

Nyambura finally accepted the inevitable and emphasized that Mwara should continue her schooling after the baby was delivered.

So Mwara accepted her fate and settled down to a simple rural life far from the madding crowd of Nairobi. She would spend her time helping Nyambura in the vegetable garden or breeding chickens, and learning how to become a responsible woman.

⚔ ⚔ ⚔

Late one evening when Juma Otieno arrived in his home town of Nyakach, his sister, Abuya, sat by the door of their late father's mud-brick house. She was a strikingly beautiful heavyset woman in her early thirties with short brown hair. She wore a knee-length dress and sandals, with a necklace of colourful plastic beads and matching earrings. An equally colourful shawl dangled from her shoulder. She welcomed his brother warmly, and promised to lend an ear to him at dawn. Her two teenage daughters, from two different relationships that went sour, and a man he had not met before greeted him. Later on in the evening, Abuya introduced the man as her boyfriend.

It was mid-morning, and they were sitting in the living room. With his heart in his mouth, Juma Otieno explained to his sister the need for them to sell the plot of land inherited from their father.

"Akeyo is suffering from a life-threatening disease," he said in a funereal tone, "and you're my only salvation."

Abuya had been quiet during Juma Otieno's apparent lamentation. It was as if the puzzle behind his request, so intriguing to her when he started to plead, had now proven too complex.

Finally, she mustered the courage to say, "My brother, haven't you heard that an oil exploration company may be coming to the community within a year or two?"

"No. I haven't heard anything like that," he replied.

"Land in this town is going to be valuable," she said firmly.

"It may all be rumours," Juma Otieno pointed out.

"I don't think so, my brother," she frowned.

"Making false promises is all the government is good at," he said.

"Why don't we wait and see?" she insisted.

"Not when Akeyo is dying," he fumed at his sister.

Throwing in the towel, Juma Otieno headed off toward the open door, out into the sunlight. Little did he think back that Kenya had become a country where women, like Abuya, Mwara and Mumbi, were celebrities who brought down men. He walked pompously, as if he was a person of importance, in possession of the conveyance to the plot of land.

A dry season's day, the hot midday sun was reminiscent of the immortal world. He felt like being roasted. He walked towards Apoko Mwai Secondary School with the hope of discussing possible employment with the principal. Once in the school's office, an indolent-looking extra-large female secretary gave him a job application form to complete. While he was doing so, she and a seemingly foolish skinny old man that worked as a messenger laughed and blabbed just about everything. Juma Otieno became more uncomfortable as she kept sucking her teeth in irritation, and moving her huge behind on a squeaky chair. The sounds grated at his nerves.

"For references, don't forget to write down the contact details of two of your former supervisors," she said with a masculine voice.

He remained silent.

Supervisors? Juma Otieno wondered who those supervisors would be, in view of his blemished reputation. Maybe, Paul Kimani and another colleague of his may serve the purpose. He quickly wrote down their contact details and handed over the form to the secretary.

"I hope you signed and dated the form," she reminded him.

"Yes, I did," he replied tersely, wanting to ask her to shut her trap.

He left the office in disgust.

Juma Otieno became a trapped man in the town of Nyakach. He felt trapped financially, emotionally, and socially. Filled with dreams for himself and Akeyo that he felt he will never realize, he spent his days moving back and forth between feeling dizzyingly optimistic and despairingly frustrated. Since he had an affair with Mwara, he knew there would come a time when there would be no one to speak to when the problems assailed him. His heart never stopped to flutter with fear.

A couple of days after his job search at Apoko Mwai Secondary School, Juma Otieno received news from Akeyo informing him about the tremendous improvement in her health condition. She had been able to settle part of her medical bills thanks to the financial support given to her by her elder brother.

⚹ ⚹ ⚹

It was not long before the police got information about Juma Otieno's attempt to find employment and his hideout. It rained buckets that morning when they came for him. He felt a burst of hot air that smelled like wet soil and mulch as they seized him by the collar of his threadbare shirt and flung him into the police van. A forest of eager eyes followed him as neighbours watched from their verandahs. He averted his gaze.

After his arrest and subsequent return to Nairobi, he was held in solitary confinement, not allowed to bathe, shave or change his clothes. He was charged with two counts of defilement. After the first court appearance, he was denied bail and remanded again in custody. Later, in the name of comradeship, Paul Kimani who had attempted to bail him took a bold step. As if to echo a line in their school song that read *Nothing material can take the place of the comradeship between you and I*, he contacted his connections in the upper echelon of society. Within a few days of going back and forth, he was able to influence the judge on behalf of Juma Otieno.

So when the case was called again, Mumbi took a seat in Nairobi Court Number 1 and waited for the truth; punishment for Juma Otieno who defiled her daughter.

Judge Ingari, a fierce-looking man, seemed ready to condemn the defendant.

"You're a disgrace to the teaching profession and to society at large," judge Ingari said sternly.

Juma Otieno, who had grown a beard in detention, bowed his head in resignation. He looked as haggard as a beggar in the Kibera slum.

The judge went on. "You acted like a He-goat who couldn't control his lust." Judge Ingari paused, his eyes blazing like fire, and then took a glance at Mumbi. He lowered his eyes onto a gold-coloured pen that he was rolling in his left hand. He continued to speak.

"I would have sentenced you to life imprisonment but because you have no criminal record, because you've also shown remorse, I hereby sentence you to fifteen years' incarceration in prison." Judge Ingari cleared his throat and added, "The sentence is suspended forthwith."

Mumbi could not believe her ears. Her heart gave a gentle leap. Has Juma Otieno just been set free? She asked herself. A flurry of anger ran through her, strong enough to take the court by surprise. And then in a rebellious manner that will be transformed in time into sad bewilderment, she shouted discordantly at the judge, "This is injustice!" Apart from a faint spasm of guilt, judge Ingari did not budge. Instead, an orderly escorted a tearful Mumbi out of the courtroom.

Two weeks later, while Juma Otieno was crossing Kenyatta Avenue in broad daylight he was hit by a truck. Unable to fully recover from the severe injuries that he sustained, he became paraplegic for the rest of his life.

In the months that followed, Mwara secretly gave birth to a baby girl. With an unflinching support from Mumbi, she was able to take care of the baby and complete her secondary school education at the Serare Uhuru School.

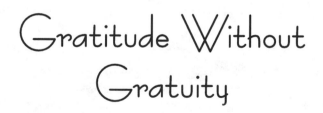

Gratitude Without Gratuity

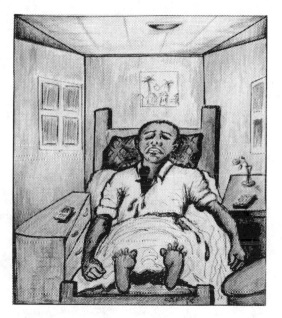

He stood at the door waiting contemplatively.

The castle-like mansion was located in a quiet luxurious area of Port Harcourt. It was mid-morning on Tuesday, August 26, 2003, the year Nigeria's elections were marred by widespread violence and outright fraud. The compound's scented garden blossomed with lush plants of roses, plumeria, and orange jasmine.

Then, Chidera Asamole made up his mind. He knocked on the door of the Ojukwus. There was no answer. He knocked louder this time. He heard footsteps inside and the door swung open. Standing there in an aggressive manner was a radiantly dark-skinned woman in her early thirties. She wore a light flowery dress. At six feet, she could have been mistaken for a wrestler. Her plump round face carried high cheekbones, big brown eyes, and fuller lips. She said:

"Yes? What do you want?"

Chidera Asamole replied quietly, touching his bowler hat.

"Is Mama Ojukwu at home?"

Chidera was a tall large man with carefully chiseled features. He looked as strong as an ox. Jet-black in complexion, he was dressed in black traditional Ijaw attire.

"Yes, but she isn't seeing anyone this morning, especially not strangers," she replied grudgingly.

"But . . .," he gasped.

"Goodbye!" she said, trying to close the door.

"Are you — Miss Ojukwu, one of the daughters?"

"Yes, I'm Ngozi Ojukwu," she replied suspiciously.

"I'm Chidera Asamole. I must talk to Mama Ojukwu about your brother," he insisted.

Ngozi Ojukwu became interested. She said, "You mean, Duru?"

"I mean, Nduka," replied Chidera.

"Nduka is dead! Go away!" said Ngozi, in a high-pitched voice.

"I have a letter here from Mr. Brown," said Chidera, waving a manila envelope. Ngozi was bewildered as she reached out for the envelope. She said:

"From Mr. Brown?"

"In Lagos?" said another feminine voice. A fair complexioned middle-aged woman who abruptly appeared behind Ngozi. Her thin narrow face glanced annoyingly at Chidera. She had the same high cheekbones as Ngozi, but her face reflected narrow eyes, broad nose, and leathery lips. She wore flattering spaghetti strap dress in black silk crepe with a splash of colour. At about five feet tall with huge fleshy behind, she reminded Chidera of the Hottentot Venus, Sarah Baartman.

Two devils in disguise, Chidera thought, and replied to them: "Yes, I'm from Mr. Brown, the solicitor in Lagos who defended Nduka."

"I'll let mother know . . .," Ngozi nodded, turned, and ran upstairs.

After a brief while, Ngozi called from up the stairs: "Let him through, Solange; mother wants him to come in."

Reluctantly, Solange moved away, as Chidera climbed the stairs towards Ngozi. She led him to a swanky-looking living room with all the paraphernalia of modern living. The house was as clean as a whistle.

Seated in one of the posh sofas was Mama Ojukwu, the opened manila envelope in her hand. A quick glance at her gave Chidera the feeling that this woman did not need to spend hundreds of naira on tanning products. Her darker skin portrayed angelic beauty, even at age sixty. She neither needed lipsticks nor lip injections to get a full set of luscious lips. She wore a natural curly, thick hair that gave her an air of superiority. Her skin, partially hidden by a beige-coloured blouse and a flannel skirt, was as smooth as silk. There probably was not a woman alive who would not want an ageless skin like that of Mama Ojukwu, Chidera thought.

"Mr. Chidera Asamole? Do sit down," she said, gesturing to a seat opposite her.

"It's kind of you to see me," said Chidera.

"Mr. Brown writes that you've news for us. Nduka wasn't liable for his conduct, I believe," said Mama Ojukwu.

Without any invitation, Ngozi joined the conversation: "Nduka was always appalling, even during childhood."

"Take it easy, my dear!" Mama Ojukwu cautioned Ngozi.

Apologetically, Ngozi responded, "I shouldn't have said that."

"It's over! Nduka was indisposed!" said Mama Ojukwu.

"I'm sorry but I don't think so," said Chidera, startling both women.

Just then a door at the other side of the room opened and a well-dressed, tall, handsome, brilliant-looking man within his forties joined them.

He said:

"Good evening, Mama Ojukwu I'm going home now. Unless, there is anything else . . .?"

"Please don't go. This is Chidera Asamole who has come to reveal to us, something about Nduka. Chidera, meet my aide, Nkem Achebe," said Mama Ojukwu.

Nkem drew a chair and sat down, showing a gleam of curiosity, Chidera thought.

"I'm here to tell you something important in spite of your insistence that the matter is closed. I would like to introduce myself as an investigative journalist for the *Nigerian Tide* newspaper. For the past twelve months, I've been away covering the Ebola virus outbreak in Uganda and Congo," said Chidera.

"Hmmm . . . another journalist," Ngozi breathed out heavily.

"Manners, please, Ngozi, manners!" cried Mama Ojukwu.

Chidera disregarded Ngozi's comment and continued speaking:

"You would agree with me that on Thursday, February 20th, 2003 at 8 p.m., Nduka was here to request for some money from his father, Papa Ojukwu. As he didn't get his way, he became intimidating. Subsequently, that same night, your husband was stabbed to death with a kitchen knife. Nduka's fingerprints were found on the knife. Not being able to come up with an alibi – at the time of the trial, he was charged and found guilty of murder. The judge sentenced him to death. He kept begging for mercy until he was taken to Apapa Lagos and executed at the Kiri Kiri Maximum Security Prison. During the trial, he was alleged to have been in the company of a man in Owerri, on the night of the murder. *I was that man!* And I can prove that Nduka was innocent."

❊ ❊ ❊

Accentuated by the perplexity of its occupants, the very air in the room froze into silence at Chidera's statement. The blow had been dealt. He could sense their alertness and distrust. Then out of the blue, Solange walked into the room with deliberation. She looked angry and did not mince words: "I just overheard! Why is this man saying that Nduka didn't commit the crime? How dare you come here and tell us such things!"

Mama Ojukwu asked the woman to take it easy. She introduced her to Chidera as Solange Tumi from Cameroon, the housekeeper who had been with her for ages. *What a bold housekeeper! She was importance personified*, he thought.

Nkem spoke for the first time: "It's best that you leave now. It's been too much for the family."

As Chidera realized that he was no longer welcome, he began to leave the room. All eyes were on him.

"I'll show you out, but you should be ashamed of yourself to have made them suffer like this!" said Solange as she and Ngozi accompanied him downstairs to the hallway.

"Chidera?" Ngozi called out. "What did you come here for?"

"For justice!" he replied.

"For justice? Nduka is dead! It's the innocent people who matter now – that's us! Can't you see what you've done to us all?" said Ngozi.

Without replying to her question, Chidera walked out of the house to the sound of the door banging behind him.

Meanwhile, in the living room upstairs, as if to console her, Nkem hugged Mama Ojukwu and quickly gave her a French kiss. She winked coquettishly at him while he glanced furtively over his shoulders to the sound of footsteps. Nkem withdrew gingerly towards the door and bade goodbye.

⚸ ⚸ ⚸

Mama Ojukwu picked up the telephone and began to dial a number as Ngozi entered the room.

"Ijeoma? It's me your mother. Something beyond the imagination has come to pass," said Mama Ojukwu over the telephone.

"What?" said Ijeoma.

"A man has turned up and confirmed to us Nduka's alibi on the night of the murder." said Mama Ojukwu.

"Was he innocent?" Ijeoma asked with a surprising tone.

"It appears so. Please come to Port Harcourt with your husband." said Mama Ojukwu, as she disconnected the call and dialled her son, Duru. She told him the news the same way as she had told her daughter. His reaction to his mother's invitation to come to Port Harcourt was one of apprehension and sarcasm.

At Ijeoma and Toyin's apartment in Owerri, the sweet smell of Ijeoma's recently prepared *egusi* soup and stock fish filled the air. But Mama Ojukwu's telephone call and the mid-morning heat had brought torment for both husband and wife. They felt like being roasted. Ijeoma was a nervous-looking average height dark-skinned woman in her late thirties. Her skinny oval-shaped face seemed to have no cheekbones. With small brown eyes darting frequently from left to right, she always seemed to be in search of something. Although her short black hair gave her some sort of empowering appearance, yet Toyin liked to remind her that her extra-thin lips would have made a mockery of her at a beauty contest.

Before she bent down to help Toyin put on his prosthetic legs, she adjusted her loose tie-dye blouse that covered her waist upon which she tied a colourful traditional wrapper. Looking at Toyin directly in the eyes, she said:

"That was mama. She wants us to go to Port Harcourt. A witness has confirmed Nduka's alibi,"

"How's that for a surprise? In that case we should get ready," said Toyin.

"Why? I've no intention of going over there now," said Ijeoma.

"Don't you realize that the case will be re-examined? Your brother will be justified, which means the crime will again be a mystery — and you're refusing to go back to Port Harcourt?" Toyin asked.

"I don't want to hear about it!" said Ijeoma.

"Wow!" responded Toyin as he struggled to keep steady on his prosthetic legs.

"Wait, let me help you," said Ijeoma.

"No, I'm fine," responded Toyin, not sounding pleased. "Whatever happens, I shall be conducting my own enquiry," said Toyin.

"What do you mean by 'enquiry'? Ijeoma asked him.

"I'll make comments that will seem harmless to everyone except the assassin, then observe people's reactions and analyse them," said Toyin.

"No Toyin, I beg you! Stay out of it," pleaded Ijeoma alarmingly to a surprised Toyin.

Toyin was born with fibular hemimelia in both legs. At one year old, his legs were amputated halfway between his knees and ankles. He had always been known for determination, eloquence, and intelligence. Since he married Ijeoma, he had been teaching Mathematics at the Holy Rosary Secondary School in Port Harcourt. Toyin looked far younger than his forty-five years. With his prosthetic legs on, he was a slim man, just shy of six feet tall. His marriage to Ijeoma was still going through the test of time, as both of them were as different as day and night.

ꭓ ꭓ ꭓ

Back in his room at the Presidential Hotel in the Government Reservation Area, Port Harcourt, Chidera was pondering over his meeting with the Ojukwus. Their reactions baffled him. Why was Ngozi so lukewarm? Why did Solange react so strongly by launching a lightning offensive?

Then the telephone rang. Chidera hastened to pick up the receiver.

"Yes?"

"Mr. Asamole? Mr. Ojukwu is asking for you in reception," said a lady's voice.

"Mr. Ojukwu? Tell him to come up," he said, a bit surprised at such an unexpected visit.

When the knock came on the door, Chidera anxiously went to open it.

"Come in. Mr. Ojukwu?" said Chidera.

"I'm Duru Ojukwu. Mr Brown gave me your contact details."

Duru's features reminded Chidera of the once-notorious Nigerian robbery kingpin, Lawrence Anni. He was a tall, lanky, dark-skinned, boyish-looking man within his mid-twenties. When he walked into the room the stench of stale sweat walked in with him. Chidera thought Duru portrayed an air of arrogance and recklessness.

"Why did you want to see me?"

"To discuss the news you brought to us about Nduka."

"But it's history for Nduka, don't you think?" said Chidera with sarcasm.

"Yes, it's too late for him. And why did you keep it to yourself for all this time?" said Duru.

"I had no way of knowing about the trial as I was out of the country. But I can assure you that Nduka was with me at a bar during the night of the murder. You should be pleased that your brother is innocent."

"Indeed, as innocent as a lamp," said Duru, sarcastically. "Except that he wasn't my brother. Furthermore, forget the idea that Papa Ojukwu was our father. We were adoptees."

His comment left Chidera dumbfounded. After a brief exchange of some more words, Duru left the room as abruptly as he came.

✘ ✘ ✘

After a while, Chidera paid a visit to Mr. Brown in his Lagos office. For Chidera's investigation, Mr. Brown had become a light in a sea of darkness and mystery.

"I'm answerable for all this. I need to know more about the Ojukwus. I'm obligated to them to find out who is to reprimand," said Chidera.

Mr. Brown paused momentarily, as if skeptical of Chidera's effort, then spoke:

"In the first place, they were all adopted. Papa Ojukwu had no children of his own. He took care of orphaned children during the Biafra war, some of whom never left."

"What was Nduka's relationship with his parents?" Chidera quietly asked Mr. Brown, watching for a change of countenance, for which he saw none.

"He was the undeniable suspect because he had always been the black sheep of the family. At school he stole from others and played truancy. He was always in debts which were settled by his parents. They forfeited everything for him. Even now, Mama Ojukwu is supporting his girlfriend."

"His girlfriend?"

"Yes, Nduka had a girlfriend called Boma Jonathan. Mama Ojukwu only found out about her the day after Nduka's arrest when she came to see her."

"I must meet her," said Chidera.

"She's now in a relationship with an oil rigger and lives in Bonny Island, where she works as a clerk for an oil company. You may also want to talk to Dr. Iroegbu, their family physician. They may tell you more about the Ojukwus," concluded Mr. Brown.

With the help of Mr. Brown's telephone calls, Chidera made appointments with Boma Jonathan and Dr. Iroegbu.

✕ ✕ ✕

At the police station on Aba Road, Port Harcourt, Superintendent Jack-May and Sergeant Dublin-Green were discussing the murder case.

"Sergeant Dublin-Green who do you think could have killed Papa Ojukwu?" said Superintendent Jack-May.

"Mama Ojukwu or Nkem Achebe could have done so, as there are rumours that they want to marry. Or maybe Solange Tumi," replied Sergeant Dublin-Green.

"Who was there at the night of the murder?" said Superintendent Jack-May.

"Mama Ojukwu and Nkem, Solange and Ngozi, Ijeoma Abbey was on a visit there with her husband Toyin Abbey. At 7:45 p.m. Papa Ojukwu was in his bedroom telling Mama Ojukwu and Nkem about his meeting with Nduka. Nkem went home just after 8 p.m. Ngozi saw his father just before 8 p.m. At 8:30 p.m. Solange found his body, during which time Mama Ojukwu was alone in her room. Taking into account that Ijeoma could have come down and killed her father during that half hour, we've five suspects. For now, let's rule out Toyin Abbey, the fellow on prosthetic legs," said Sergeant Dublin-Green.

"Papa Ojukwu could have let someone into the house. Mama Ojukwu said that she heard the door bell, followed by the front door closing. Maybe it was the other son, Duru?" said Superintendent Jack-May.

"Who knows? Maybe you're right," said Sergeant Dublin-Green. Finally, it was agreed that Sergeant Dublin-Green should interview members of the family.

⚶ ⚶ ⚶

Outside the office of an oil company at Rumumasi, Port Harcourt, Chidera met Nduka's former girlfriend, Boma Jonathan. The scorching midday sun reflected an unattractive-looking woman. Her large liquid brown eyes held such an ignorance and agitation that it was impossible for him not to notice them. Her cheekbones were not especially high and her nose was a little too flat, hence the uncertain disproportion of her facial features. Remarkably short in height, she wore her thick, black hair in cornrows. The nauseating stench of skin-bleaching cream coming from her skin sent Chidera's nose on a twitching jive.

"Boma? I'm Chidera; I would like to talk to you about Nduka Ojukwu."

She painstakingly explained to Chidera that she started disassociating herself from Nduka while he was in prison. She said that Nduka was a ladies' man. That on several occasions he used his charm to swindle people out of their money. That the day after his arrest, she went to Mama Ojukwu and informed her that she was his son's girlfriend. As far as Boma was concerned, he could well have been guilty of murder. At the end of their conversation, Chidera concluded that Boma was truly a garrulous person, although she gave him worthwhile information.

⚝ ⚝ ⚝

Even though he felt exhausted under the scorching midday sun, Chidera took a taxi to meet Dr. Iroegbu at his clinic. For about one hour, the taxi found itself in a massive traffic jam. Swarmed by people and vehicles, the apocalyptic scene on the main road reflected the city's urban problems. Vehicles were wedged bumper-to-bumper in both directions. The atmosphere was charged with curses and horn blasts piercing the diesel exhaust–choked air. Engines that could not cope coughed, grunted, and collapsed in the moribund road system.

Dr. Iroegbu, a short fair-complexioned man, was sitting hunched over a bunch of papers when he finally met him. He got to his feet to greet Chidera. He looked like someone in his early sixties though it turned out he was only fifty-five years old. An appearance left by years in the sun. Clearing his throat, he managed to find a voice: "Pleased to meet you," he croaked weakly, and gave Chidera a knowing smile.

"Thank you. It's a pleasure meeting you too. Could you please tell me what you know about Papa Ojukwu?" said Chidera.

Dr. Iroegbu rubbed his nose and said, "Well, he was a very concerned father. As a result, his wife was left in the background. His children were pampered. He seemed as if he wanted to control their lives. I wasn't surprised that Nduka could bring himself to kill him."

"Even so none of the children had any motive," said Chidera.

"Not at first glance, but if you think twice . . . ," he paused, as a frown creased his face. "They were dependent on Papa Ojukwu financially, and they didn't seem to like his control over them."

"I learnt that Ijeoma got married to Toyin against the advice of her father," said Chidera.

"Yes," said Dr. Iroegbu, excitedly. "As for Ngozi, she became infatuated with Nollywood and fell in love with a glamorous movie star. You know the Ramsey Nouah-type. Abandoned by him and with no talent as an actress, she was forced against her wishes to return home."

"What about Duru?"

"Duru never came to terms with being abandoned by his biological parents. Ungratefully, he sorely hated Papa Ojukwu. He became an importer of used clothing to avoid the law career marked out for him by his father. And the Cameroonian housekeeper, Solange Tumi, also disliked Papa Ojukwu because I heard that he once tried to seduce her."

"Is it true that Mama Ojukwu is about to marry her husband's aide, Nkem?" said Chidera.

"It's amazing how she discreetly goes about her extra-marital affair. However, Papa Ojukwu's death did simplify matters a great deal," concluded Dr. Iroegbu, with an undisguised leer.

"Until we explain who's responsible for his murder, the whole family's loyalty to him will be held in question," said Chidera.

✕ ✕ ✕

Within the same week, the police conducted an interview in the dismal house. It was mid-morning as members of the Ojukwus gathered in the living room. Sergeant Dublin-Green made the opening remarks:

"Following the confirmation of Nduka's alibi, the public prosecutors' office had decided to re-examine the case. Time has elapsed since the incident; hence your memories will no longer be fresh in your minds. However, a detail that was insignificant at the time could by now have assumed a vital importance."

Mama Ojukwu was asked to make a comment:

"At around 7:45 p.m. my late husband had come upstairs to tell us that, as had happened on previous occasions, Nduka had attempted to blackmail him into giving him money. He had refused."

"Did Nduka then leave?" asked Sergeant Dublin-Green.

"Yes, definitely," replied Mama Ojukwu.

"Nkem, what happened after that?" said Sergeant Dublin-Green.

"Mama Ojukwu said I could leave. I packed up my things and left at around 8:00 p.m.," said Nkem.

"Did you pass by Papa Ojukwu's bedroom?" said Sergeant Dublin-Green.

"Yes, the door was ajar, but I didn't want to go in as I assumed Papa Ojukwu was busy," said Nkem.

"If you had opened the door, would you have seen the body?" said Sergeant Dublin-Green.

"Yes, I realize that now," said Nkem.

"Mama Ojukwu, can you confirm that you heard the doorbell a few moments after your late husband went to his bedroom?" said Sergeant Dublin- Green.

"Yes, but I don't remember the exact time," said Mama Ojukwu.

"Did you know that Nduka was having a relationship?" said Sergeant Dublin- Green.

"Certainly not! I was doubtful when Solange came to tell me that a girl had turned up claiming to be Nduka's girlfriend. You were surprised, weren't you, Solange?" said Mama Ojukwu.

"I couldn't believe it! I made her repeat herself before I could let her in. It was unbelievable!" said Solange.

"Ngozi, what were you doing?" said Sergeant Dublin-Green.

"I helped Solange to clean the kitchen," Ngozi replied.

"That's right. Then you went up to your room, only coming out later on to go and see a play in Aggry," added Solange.

"In any case, why are you asking me all this when it's already written in your notebooks?" said Ngozi, drawing her eyebrows together in an expression of intense contempt.

Sergeant Dublin-Green dismissed her question, and said: "What time did you go out? Did you see Papa Ojukwu?"

"Before leaving at 8 p.m., I went to ask him for some money which he gave me. Afterwards, Solange and I left at almost precisely the same time," said Ngozi.

"Now then, Solange, why don't you tell us about what you remember?" said Sergeant Dublin- Green.

"After having cleaned the kitchen, Ngozi went up to her room. Then Nduka arrived. I let him in as he had forgotten his key. He went straight to see his late father, and I went back to the kitchen. After a while, he left again shouting about something. Papa Ojukwu was in the hall. He went upstairs to talk to his wife and I left for a stroll in the garden. When I returned at around 8:30 p.m., I found Papa Ojukwu dead. The knife was on the ground, and the drawers of the desk were pulled out," said Solange, averting the sergeant's gaze.

"And you, Ijeoma, what were you doing by then?" said Sergeant Dublin-Green.

"We were in our room. We didn't hear anything, until Solange screamed," said Ijeoma.

"And you Duru?" said Sergeant Dublin-Green.

"I was alone in my shop sorting out goods," said Duru.

"Mama Ojukwu, it seems as though money is the key to this. Nduka insisted that your late husband had given him the money, and yet he told you that this wasn't the case. So where did he get it from? Did you give it to him Solange?" said Sergeant Dublin- Green.

"No, the money was in a drawer that Papa Ojukwu locked," said Solange.

"Did you give it to him Ngozi?" said Sergeant Dublin-Green.

"No, Nduka had already gone!" she responded furiously.

"Oh! I thought you didn't know when he left?" said Sergeant Dublin-Green.

"I know now, I didn't then. Anyway, I wouldn't have given Nduka anything," said Ngozi.

As Mama Ojukwu accompanied Sergeant Dublin-Green to the door, he said, "Now we can presume that your late husband did give Nduka the money, as Nduka told us at the time. Then he must have been telling the truth."

✄ ✄ ✄

Back in his hotel room, Chidera was having a nap when the telephone rang.

"Hello? Chidera speaking . . . Mama Ojukwu? What do you mean? Toyin is dead? He has been stabbed? Duru Ojukwu has been detained? What? The knife that stabbed Toyin was found in Duru's pocket? Thanks for letting me know. I'm on my way."

Chidera replaced the receiver and murmured to himself. "I know who the murderer is!"

At the Ojukwus, he was welcomed by Mama Ojukwu.

"Thank you for coming Chidera," said Mama Ojukwu.

"It's my pleasure. I must talk to you all," said Chidera.

"Haven't you done enough harm yet? All this is your fault!" shouted Ijeoma.

"I must finish what I started," said Chidera.

"Tell us! You must tell us if you know something, even though it won't bring back Toyin," said Ijeoma.

"Life's so unjust! It's like for my late husband's unrelenting gratitude, he receives no gratuity," said Mama Ojukwu.

"Now I understand why your reaction to me when I first arrived was so surprising it wasn't at all what I expected. You had all come to terms with the idea that Nduka was guilty. You had even been able to excuse his actions. Nduka was the type of guy who enlisted others to do his dirty job. He used someone else to kill Papa Ojukwu while he went out of the house so he could prove he was elsewhere. He was the ringleader of the crime . . . Isn't that right Solange?" said Chidera.

"I don't know! But why would you think that?" cried Solange.

"He seduced you, just as he had seduced other women," said Chidera.

"That's rubbish!" shouted Solange, as her eyes glinted resentfully.

"After he seduced you, he asked you to steal the money of Papa Ojukwu. Then he drove you to murder him. The next day when his girlfriend Boma arrived, you despised him all the more. And Toyin was becoming a menace, so you had to get rid of him. The one thing you had left to do was to slip the knife into Duru's pocket, after having wiped off your fingerprints," concluded Chidera.

"Is this true, Solange?" said Mama Ojukwu.

"No . . . It was Nduka! He was the guilty one, not me. He betrayed me!" said Solange. She drew in sharp angry breaths and stood like one stunned. Her heart must be thumping hard against her ribs, Chidera thought.

"Arghh! Let me at her! Let me . . . she killed Toyin!" screamed Ijeoma, rushing at Solange, as Mama Ojukwu held Ijeoma back.

Solange began to run away from them, as she became the focus of attention.

"Quick . . . she's escaping!" shouted Ngozi.

"Let her go, Ngozi. The police are outside . . . she can't escape," said Chidera.

10

The Monrovia Woman

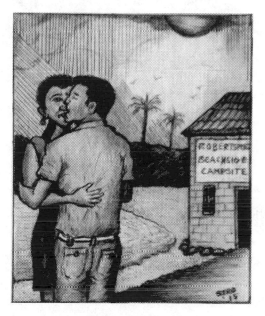

At ten in the morning, police detective Samuel Tubman's cell phone rang.

"Hello? Hello?"

"Hello, is that you, Tubman?"

"Yes, that's me."

"Police Inspector Kromah speaking here. "

"How can I help you my friend?"

"There is a suicide at the Montserrado County area of Monrovia. Bungalow number fifty-five. A man in his forties . . . A Mr. Broh. Would you like to come with me?"

"Surely I'll come."

Tubman, in his mid-fifties, was a hefty dark-complexioned man with a small head that looked big because of his jet-black Afro-styled hair. His was fully-bearded.

Both Tubman and Kromah arrived at house number 55 almost together. They quickly jumped out their cars and entered the bungalow where police Sergeant Conneh was waiting.

He gave the two men a briefing:

"Deceased is a Mr. Broh, sir. He lived here with a friend — a Mr. Doe. A houseboy called Titus comes in daily to work. Mr. Doe was away in Gbarnga, Bong County, and returned this morning. He called and knocked on Mr. Broh's door which was locked on the inside, but he received no response. He got worried and called the police at about nine o'clock. We came and opened the door only to find Mr. Broh on the floor shot through the head. There was a Browning Hi-Power 9mm semi-automatic pistol in his hand."

"Where are Mr. Doe and Titus?"

"They are in one of the bedrooms, sir."

"I'll talk to him and then George. Firstly, let me talk to George."

Tubman and Kromah joined George, the doctor, and Sergeant Taylor in the deceased's bedroom. The body of a man in his forties was lying on the floor close to a chair. He was a tall man, dressed in a dark suit with no tie, and black shoes. He had short curly hair, and handsome facial features. His left hand was still wrapped around a pistol, and on the right side of his head was blood.

"What do you have to say, doctor?" Inspector Kromah asked.

The doctor gave the men a quick glance and said:

"If you take a close look, you'll notice that he isn't really holding the pistol. And even though the pistol is in his left hand, the bullet wound is on the right side of the head. He was killed at about half past eight last night."

"It looks like someone is trying to make this look like a case of suicide," said Inspector Kromah.

"The key to the room's locked door can't be traced, and the windows were closed, sir," added Sergeant Taylor.

"It's interesting that no suicide letter was found," said Tubman.

"Let's go see what Mr. Doe has for us," said Inspector Kromah.

✳ ✳ ✳

Tubman and Kromah moved over to the bedroom where two men were waiting for them. One of them, probably in his thirties, had an athletic build. He was a fair in complexion bald-headed person who looked intelligent, thought Tubman. The other man was dark smallish and shabby-looking with thick black dreadlocks. He looked no more than twenty-two years old.

Inspector Kromah addressed the man who looked like an athlete:

"Mr. Doe?"

"Yes, I am. And this is Titus our houseboy."

The inspector then asked Sergeant Taylor to take a statement from Titus while he introduced himself to Mr. Doe.

"I'm Inspector Kromah. Now, tell me what you know."

"I entered the house this morning at about eight forty-five, and Titus wasn't yet at work, although he starts work at eight. I went to my bedroom before knocking on the door of Monon-Konmlan, I mean Mr. Broh. As there was no response, I called the police, because they should be the one to call if anything was wrong."

"Why did you think that something was wrong?" Kromah asked.

"I was acting on a hunch."

"Can you think of any reason for Mr. Doe to have committed suicide?"

"Not to my knowledge."

"Did you know he had a pistol?"

"Yes, I did."

"Could you please tell me more about him?"

"I came to know Monon-Konmlan three years ago when I was searching for a job. He recommended me to a couple of people who were helpful in my search. We became close friends and decided to stay together."

Doe stopped talking until Kromah asked:

"Do you know anything more about him?"

"He had a wife who disappeared during the civil war. He had no children."

"Was he having financial problems?"

"I don't think so."

"Had Mr. Broh any girlfriend?"

"He had one called Jayplo Weah who lives here in Montserrado County."

Doe hesitated and then said: "He had another girlfriend we fondly referred to as the Monrovia woman. She is called Miatta Johnson and lives in the lower Johnsonville, Montserrado County area of Monrovia."

"When did you last see Mr. Broh?"

"Thursday last, before I went for the weekend."

"And you went to . . .?"

"I went to Gbarnga, Bong County."

"Whom did you go there to see?"

"I went to see my friend, Emmanuel Flomo."

"And you returned early this morning."

"Yes, I did."

Tubman decided to ask some questions.

"What do you think of Jayplo Weah?"

Doe hesitated as if the question made him uncomfortable, then he replied.

"She is beautiful, but she looks like a free woman who thinks too much of herself."

"And what do you think of Miatta Johnson?"

"She is very rich, and not so nice."

"Was there any misunderstanding between you and Monon-Konmlan?"

"There was none."

"Do you know why anybody would want to kill him?"

"I don't know. It could be anybody - Miatta Johnson, Jayplo Weah, one of his relatives or friends. Anybody."

"It looks like there was no reason to make him commit suicide," said Inspector Kromah, as he left Tubman and Doe to join Sergeant Taylor in the other room.

✕ ✕ ✕

Tubman felt that Doe was not at ease. So he tried to sound more pleasant in questioning Doe.

"So, you didn't expect Monon-Konmlan to commit suicide."

"No, I didn't. Even if he did commit suicide, I can't picture him killing himself that way."

"Why wouldn't he have done it that way?"

"Well, sometime ago, after watching a movie together about suicide he said if ever he's to do so, he would prefer slashing his wrist in a bucket of water.

"And what was your own preference?"

"I told him I'll prefer shooting myself. But I still can't believe he committed suicide."

"It might be murder," said Tubman.

Doe looked dumbfounded and hesitated before saying,

"I don't think so because the windows and door were locked on the inside."

"But the key is missing."

"Maybe it's somewhere in his bedroom."

"The bedroom will be searched."

"Now I see. It could be murder," said Doe, quietly.

"Do you know why somebody would want to kill him?" asked Tubman, closely watching Doe's facial expression.

"I don't know," said Doe, in an unconvincing manner.

Inspector Kromah entered the room and walked towards Doe to show him a locket.

"Mr. Doe, have you ever seen this before?"

"I've never seen it before," he said shaking his head.

✕ ✕ ✕

In Monon-Konmlan's bedroom, Kromah and Tubman were discussing their findings as the body had been photographed and removed.

"Doe might have killed him. We'll have to check his alibi," said Kromah.

"Maybe they had a brawl over that girlfriend, Jayplo Weah," said Tubman.

"That's right. I noticed that he was critical in his remarks about her."

"He definitely knows something that he's withholding from us." Tubman scratched his head deliberately before asking. "Did you find any fingerprints?"

"There were none on the pistol, neither anywhere else of any other person, apart from those of the deceased."

"Fantastic! Wouldn't it be a great newspaper headline? *Dead Man Wiped Pistol.*"

"Indeed, and Titus, the houseboy, told Sergeant Taylor that Monon-Konmlan and Doe were cordial to each other."

Inspector Kromah searched the deceased's room and came up with a bank book. It showed that the deceased withdrew several large sums of money within the past fortnight. It also showed an overdraft.

Sergeant Taylor reported that none of the neighbours heard a gunshot. At least one woman, Musu Konneh, believed Monon-Konmlan was at home most of the day. Later in the day, she saw an athletic-looking woman entering Monon-Konmlan's house. According to Musu, the woman seemed to be a fair-complexioned person in her forties. The woman left soon after, seen off by him at the doorstep. That was about fifteen minutes past eight.

⌘ ⌘ ⌘

Inspector Kromah and Tubman approached Mr. Doe once more for questioning inside Bungalow number 55.

"Mister, it's time to let the cat out of the bag," said Kromah.

"Haven't I answered your questions?" Doe inquired impatiently.

"Yes, you have. But do you know of a fair-complexioned athletic-looking woman in her forties who paid Monon-Konmlan a visit last night."

"It could have been Miatta Johnson."

"You mean the other girlfriend?"

"Yes, the other girlfriend of Monon-Konmlan until Jayplo Weah came into the scene."

"Would it surprise you if I say Miatta Johnson was blackmailing Monon-Konmlan?" asked Tubman.

"I would agree with you. Lately, Monon-Konmlan wasn't comfortable with her."

"I would have expected Monon-Konmlan to have killed Miatta Johnson, and not the other way round," said Tubman.

"Maybe there was a fight between them which led to him being shot, and then she tried to make it look like suicide," Doe suggested.

"But somebody saw Monon-Konmlan seeing Miatta Johnson off at the doorstep."

Doe was taken aback. He became speechless for a while before saying: "But she might have come back later."

"That's true," said Tubman.

Inspector Kromah decided to have a look in a small storeroom that was not searched earlier.

Mr. Doe said:

"It's locked."

"Yes," said Kromah, glancing at Doe distrustfully. Can I get the key?"

Doe froze, looking confused.

"I can't remember where it is."

Kromah looked at Tubman expectantly before saying: "We can try to open it."

Doe shifted onward rigidly.

"Wait," he said. "It should be . . ."

He went across the room to a set of drawers and fished out a key. Kromah took the key and opened the storeroom. It had a window from which a ray of sunlight penetrated into the room. There was a sizable amount of junk in the room. On the top of a table was a briefcase.

As Kromah reached out to pick it up, Doe said hastily:

"It belongs to me."

"Can I take a look?" asked Kromah.

Hesitantly, Doe replied, "Yes."

The briefcase was unlatched. Inside it were toiletries. There were a couple of newspapers in it but nothing else.

Kromah shut the lid, and slowly inspected the storeroom. Once done, he gave the key back to Doe and asked him:

"Can you give me Jayplo Weah's address?"

"She is at number sixteen Ashmond Street."

"Thank you, Mr. Doe. We may like to meet with you later."

As they left the house, Kromah asked Tubman:

"What do you think?"

"He's definitely hiding something from us."

✄ ✄ ✄

A couple of days later, Kromah and Tubman met for drinks at the Robertsport Beach Campsite. Kromah was saying:

"I've checked on Doe's friend, Emmanuel Flomo in Gbarnga, Bong County. Flomo confirmed that Doe spent part of the weekend with him."

"He could be lying," said Tubman.

"He could be. Moreover, why do you think Doe was all worked up when I searched the briefcase?"

As usual, Tubman scratched his head deliberately before replying: "That's another puzzle we'll have to solve."

Kromah moved to another topic.

"On the other hand, Jayplo Weah will be coming to see me at my office in two hours".

"Well, I hope you'll get some useful information from her."

"And we now know where Miatta Johnson is living. You might want to join me in the interview."

"That's fine with me."

Jayplo Weah was on time for her appointment with Inspector Kromah. She was a beautiful fair complexion young woman of medium height. Full-figured, large brown eyes and a chubby face, she had that Oprah Winfrey looks.

"Jayplo Weah, I'm so sorry about all this, and thanks for coming," said Kromah.

"It's okay, Inspector. But why would he have committed suicide?"

"That's the question. Was there any misunderstanding between you?"

"No," Jayplo replied dismissively.

"Well, it was murder or suicide."

"Murder?" Jayplo's eyes showed surprise. "Did you say murder?"

"That's right. Tell me, who do you think might want to kill Monon-Konmlan?"

"As far as I know, nobody might want to do such horrible thing to him."

"He had a pistol. Did you know that?"

"Not to my knowledge."

"What do you think of Mr. Doe?"

"He appears to be a good person, although not my kind of man."

"I see," said Kromah. "Do you know Miatta Johnson?"

"Miatta? Miatta? Yes. I met her once at Monon-Konmlan's. Again, like Mr. Doe, not my kind of woman."

"Jayplo Weah, where were you on the night of the murder?"

"Hmmm, where was I? Yes. . . .Now I know. I was at home until about eight o'clock when I left for a walk."

"And you returned home at what time?"

"I'm not sure. Maybe, I might have returned between half past eight and nine."

Kromah rose and shook her hands. "That's all for now. I might call on you again. Thank you."

✖ ✖ ✖

Miatta Johnson received Kromah and Tubman with absolute confidence. The men introduced themselves.

Her house was of enormous size and comfortable. She lived the lifestyles of the rich and famous in the lower Johnsonville, Montserrado County area of Monrovia. She was living the high life with the likes of Miatta Fambuleh. Miatta Johnson grew to like the well-to-do life. She liked spending money, meeting celebrities.

Kromah asked her:

"Do you know why we're here?"

Miatta shook her head unemotionally. She was a short fair complexion athletic-looking woman in her forties. She looked attractive with large brown eyes, slightly broad nose, and prominent lips. A short black wig sat on her head like a hat. Like the Greek goddess Aphrodite, Miatta was a gorgeous, perfect, eternally young woman with a beautiful body. It was said that her girdle gave her magical powers to maintain a potent sexual attractiveness and compelling love. Some thought that she was a bit stuck on herself. But with a perfect face and body, who can blame her? She could lure anybody.

She said:

"No, I don't know why you're here."

"You might have heard about what happened with Monon-Konmlan whom you know."

"Yes, indeed. That's too bad for him."

"Did you also know his wife?"

Miatta appeared doubtful before responding:

"No, I never knew her. But I heard that he disappeared during the civil war."

"How close were you to Monon-Konmlan?"

"We were just friends."

"We know that you visited Monon-Konmlan. Can you tell us what happened while you were there?"

"I was there at about half past seven. We sat and talked."

"Where in the house did you sit with him?"

"We sat in the living room, and I left at about a quarter past eight."

"You didn't enter Monon-Konmlan's bedroom?"

"No, I didn't."

"Did you misplace your locket of late?"

"No."

"We found a locket in Monon-Konmlan's bedroom."

"I don't know anything about that," said Miatta with a quivering voice.

"You may have to come with us for further interrogation," concluded Inspector Kromah.

"Why are you trying to get me into trouble?" asked Miatta, as tears ran down her cheeks.

Miatta Johnson grew up poor. She had a terrible childhood. Her mother was a prostitute, and her father was an alcoholic who sexually abused her. When her parents abandoned her she was brought up in foster homes. By the time Miatta was twenty-five she was bright, attractive and well-liked. She was, according to her friends, a nice, friendly person who would hurt no one.

She was lucky to marry a wealthy Liberian businessman and politician commonly called Uncle. He was a staunch member of the Americo-Liberian ethnic group's True Whig Party. His political party had monopolized power since independence in 1847 until 1980, when a coup d'état created insecurity that led to a 14-year civil war.

Uncle's worth had been estimated at three million dollars, a fortune which he invested in real estate in Monrovia. He also traded in scrap metal. He had the Hephaestus' appearance: a dark-haired man who had difficulty walking due to deformed feet. He was smaller in stature, creative, cunning, and vindictive. Uncle was known to be unable to handle his liquor.

As Uncle and Miatta had no children, they adopted an underprivileged girl from a village. The girl died mysteriously at the age of ten. Uncle bequeathed his wealth to Miatta before he passed away. She had achieved her dream of conquering poverty. Her next dream was that of having a good companion as a husband. Then she met and fell in love with Monon-Konmlan by chance. And when she saw that dream being snatched away from her she apparently turned to revenge.

❊ ❊ ❊

The next day, after making an appointment with Mr. Doe, Inspector Kromah and Tubman met him once again at Bungalow number 55. The three men were seated around a table.

"Miatta Johnson has been arrested," said Tubman, "we're bringing together evidence with regards to the murder."

Doe looked anxiously from Kromah to Tubman, rubbing his unshaven chin.

"Mr. Doe, the truth is that you found Monon-Konmlan lying dead and you decided to hurt Miatta Johnson who refused to be your girlfriend. You took the pistol, wiped it and place it in the right hand. You were lucky to find Miatta's locket which you left there as an evidence. You then closed the window and locked the door before calling the police. You refused at first to say anything but you suggested doubts of suicide. Later you were anxious to set us on the trail of Miatta Johnson."

Mr. Doe jumped to his feet.

"The Monrovia woman, I mean Miatta Johnson, pushed Monon-Konmlan to his death! All was fine when she supported him financially and morally. Then he started dating Jayplo Weah, and Miatta became angry and jealous. She asked him to return most of the money that she had been giving him or else she would inform the police that he sold his wife during the war. Hence she started blackmailing him."

Tubman said to Doe: "Your friend died, in the last resort, because he had not the courage to live."

He paused.

"And you? Do you really wish to destroy the life of anybody?"

He stared at him. His eyes darkened. Suddenly he muttered:

"No. You're right. I don't. But my wish was that Miatta or Jayplo should fall in love with me. While Miatta was sponsoring Monon-Konmlan, Jayplo was fleecing him. She and Monon-Konmlan were thrilled to have financial security from Miatta. He was far older than Jayplo. He put her through accounting school and helped her in other business ventures like trading in monkey meat."

Both Kromah and Tubman were listening attentively until Tubman interrupted Doe, "So when did you become so jealous?"

"I became more jealous when Miatta and Monon-Konmlan started talking about getting married."

"I see. Please carry on," said Tubman.

Doe continued:

"Monon-Konmlan gave Jayplo nice, expensive things. They frequently went to Robertsport."

"You mean the coastal town with excellent surfing opportunities, comfortable holiday lodges and a beach-side campsite?" Kromah inquired.

"Yes. But why should I be telling you all this?" Doe questioned himself. Shyly, he bowed his head.

Then, turning on his heel, he went swiftly from the room.

Inspector Kromah looked at Tubman for a while and said:

"This is not a case of murder disguised as suicide, but suicide made to look like murder."

11

Refuge In Banjul

Was it not Wednesday, January 27, 1999, three weeks after the rebel invasion of Freetown that you decided to flee the country? On your own volitions, you, Evelyn Gendemeh, decided to call that harmattan day Kontorfeely – The Day of Kontorfeely. You recalled fully well how in the coolness of dusk a little wind was blowing in from the mountains bringing the sound of bombs and gun fire to Government Wharf. You and Emmanuel Fallah, your boyfriend, could hardly move in the seemingly narrow corridor of escape with a sea of frightened people. They cried, screamed, and cursed so loudly that it could wake a deaf person on the other side of Mount Aureol. They all had one aim: to force their way through the gate of the wharf and join the cargo ship, *MV Madame Monique*. It was like crossing the gates to heaven from hell.

Although you knew that the ship was heading to Banjul, The Gambia, yet you also realized that most of the people in the crowd do not even know where they were going. At first, Emmanuel was unconvinced about leaving town because of his ailing mother, Dora. You too had been wondering whether to run away from the civil war or to continue staying in town with your elder brother, Charles. However, in the past couple of days, while you and Emmanuel were suffering in the throes of hell, a strange instinct urged you to take refuge in Banjul.

"We must leave this place," you confided to Emmanuel.

You still wondered though if, once in Banjul, you would get the United Nations High Commissioner for Refugees (UNHCR) registration card and the chance to resettle with your twin sister, Joyce, in Brisbane, Australia. Then, you plan to sponsor Emmanuel to join you in the Land Down Under.

It was on that Day of Kontorfeely you realized the futility of human endeavour in a doomed society. It was that day that you and Emmanuel were carrying suitcases on your head waving for help from Captain Sesay, the naval officer at Government Wharf. The short dark-complexioned captain dressed in white navy uniform noticed your desperately waving hand and asked the soldiers manning the gate to let you into the harbour.

In your early thirties, athletic-looking and elegant, you had a piercing gaze behind your horn-rimmed glasses. You were an intelligent woman, with a sober, calm dynamism: a banker at the National Commercial Bank. But on that Day of Kontorfeely, you had panic etched on your face. You were afraid that heaven would tumble down on you and everybody else struggling to board the *MV Madame Monique*.

As you paid for the fare for both yourself and Emmanuel, you poked him, suppressing your joy, knowing that you have surmounted a major hurdle. In his late thirties, you liked him as a boyfriend for many good reasons. One of them being that he fulfilled to the letter his obligations. Tall, elegant, calm, he looked perpetually relaxed, even in moments of crisis. His demands were few and momentary. But in the last couple of weeks, he had lost so much weight that the over-large shirt he was wearing made his neck stick out. In the eyes of some people, he may have reflected the image of a discreet man with no status or fortune. But for you, Emmanuel, a secondary school teacher of African History, was a sweetheart. Envied by other men, he basked in your adoring eyes. Your devotion to him was legendary. Your kind was a rarity.

While on board, you were not surprised to find out that the ship was over-crowded with men, women, and children fleeing from a city where they lived with the dead and with death all around them. You heard someone saying mockingly, "even the bankers are running away." And you knew she was referring to you. But her comment did not bother you as you were reminded of the legendary Baule tale of a war with the Ashantis.

The Ashantis pursued the Baules like animals to a wide river. In the absence of a bridge, the Baules asked the crocodiles to help them across. The crocodiles complied, but in return they demanded the most beloved possession of the Baules. In tears, the queen gave them her only son. Then the crocodiles queued side by side in the river and the Baules walked across their backs to safety. Evelyn Gendemeh, Emmanuel Fallah and the other passengers, in your eyes, were the Baules while the fighters were the Ashantis.

As the ship rolled on her moorings, enveloped by the salty smell of the sea, its captain's promise to set sail that night was never fulfilled. He was lying shamelessly. The ship left the harbour at dusk of the next day. By then, there was no more water on board let alone food. Whenever you attempt to make use of the toilets, the penetrating stench of urine, feces and vomit made you to run away as though death was at your heels. You felt like someone forcibly plunged into sadness and uncertainty.

⚒ ⚒ ⚒

Within about fifteen minutes into the voyage, the old struggling engine of the ship and the eerie sound of seagulls against the background of a moonless night made you feel like returning home. But where was home? Was it not supposed to be a place of peace, tranquility and security? Surely, home would not be a place where within the past couple of weeks your life had been as close to intolerable as human life can get. Neither would home be where people whom you should have been able to trust had turned against you. Your face darkened suddenly as you thought of your suffering in the last few weeks. And so you quickly made up your mind to continue the voyage. In reality, the captain would not turn back the ship just for your sake. If it came to making a choice, you preferred dying at sea than on a land that was under siege by soldiers and rebel fighters.

As the ship's engine continued to back-fire, a visible flame momentarily shot out of its funnel causing a popping noise. The ship lost power and forward motion. It began to roll from side to side as the waves tossed it like a large bobbing cork, dead in the sea. The ship's breakdown became a harbinger of turmoil. You stared at Emmanuel with fear. He shut his eyes and opened them, shaking his head incredulously. For the first time since you left Freetown, your eyes filled with tears. But you quickly came to realize that despair at that moment was a luxury to which the displaced were not entitled.

You started to count the minutes and the hours as the night went on. Plunged in dark patches of eternity, you were afraid of breathing too noisily. You fell asleep, only to be awakened by the sound of the ship's engine and forward propulsion. And then that thrilling taste of happiness engulfed you with a sweet-burning sensation. Emmanuel told you that the ship's crew had done the repairs by improvising on the spot.

"I guess they chose from that amazing range of human creativity," he marvelled.

You thought they must have adjusted quickly to changes after realizing that the future survival of all on board depended on them. Within the past few weeks, hope was what kept you going in the face of the most overwhelming obstacles and dangers. The exhilarating moment you have been waiting for had arrived as the ship began to sail again. You fell asleep once more. Banjul, here you come, as happiness and uncertainty beckoned.

⚹ ⚹ ⚹

As you woke up, the early morning sunlight penetrated painfully into your eyes. Emmanuel, who appeared not to have slept at all, informed you that the ship may not be allowed to enter the port of Banjul. He heard rumours from some passengers that your ship's captain was worried the Gambian authorities had no knowledge of his arrival. Already, emergency medical treatment was needed by passengers, especially children and a couple of pregnant women.

Once the ship entered Gambian territorial waters, it was met by the country's coast guards. They ordered your ship's captain to move his vessel back into international waters and await further instructions. So you spent the night anchored out at sea while being battered by strong winds from the Sahara Desert. You and Emmanuel could hardly explain how you managed for the rest of the night without food and water. Fortunately, time went by so fast.

At dawn, you saw some fishermen in their canoes throwing loaves of bread and sachets of water to desperate passengers on the ship. You admired the bravery of these Good Samaritan fishermen. You stood transfixed as you watched Emmanuel struggle with others to grab some food. Old and young, men, women, and children pushed and shoved each other. There was a man among them whom you knew to be a well-to-do businessman in Freetown. Emmanuel stood his ground. His arms were like immovable logs, and his clenched fingers were as certain as a death grip. As he brought you some food and water, his eyes rolled up to latch with yours, and he said, "I love you." You responded with a smile as your eyes, perpetually hidden behind horn-rimmed glasses, shone and twinkled like stars in the galaxy.

By late morning, orders were given to the ship's captain to anchor his vessel in the port of Banjul. The jubilant spell that ran through the passengers on hearing this news was cut short when they were loaded like cattle into police and the United Nations High Commission for

Refugees (UNHCR) trucks. You were separated from Emmanuel as women and children were placed in trucks different from those in which the men found themselves. Those that needed urgent medical treatment were taken to the city's Royal Victoria Teaching Hospital while the rest of you were driven in a convoy to the Basse refugee camp, several kilometres away. Emmanuel and the other men were taken away to an unknown destination. You heard rumours the Gambian authorities were suspicious that rebel fighters may be among the men.

En route to the refugee camp, the UNHCR truck in which you found yourself got into an accident. In an attempt to avoid a bull crossing the road, the truck veered off into a ditch. It became immobile. Blowing like a whale, you yelled bloody murder. Luckily for you and the other passengers, nobody suffered any serious injury. With a small sigh of relief, you blamed the driver for over-speeding on a small road full of potholes. Later, you were all then squeezed like sardines in a tin onto another UNHCR truck that was in the convoy.

✕ ✕ ✕

On arrival at the Basse refugee camp late in the evening, you were surprised to see a large number of people, mainly Sierra Leoneans and Liberians, living in a sprawl of tents. You were initially registered by the UNHCR and accommodated by its camp officials in one of the tents in which some women were living. A couple of them grunted disdainfully and complained about the tight sleeping quarters. Or is it that they did not like your looks in the horn-rimmed glasses? Dismayed by your lodging, you wondered about the whereabouts of Emmanuel whom you thought to be incredibly handsome for something terrible to happen to him. With no will to do anything, you drifted on the waves of tiredness and slept through the night.

In the morning, your interest in anything new and foreign to your experience became intense. You observed that the camp had a high number of teenagers and children. Prostitution was rife among the refugees and sexual exploitation by some Non-Government

Organization workers was not uncommon in the camp. You learnt that once the majority of adult refugees were registered under the UNHCR, they preferred living out of the camp. Their choices of residence were Serekunda, and Bakau. Others found themselves in the Koudoum refugee camp or in places like Tipperage, and Bundung. Serekunda was a larger town known for its market, its silk cotton tree and its wrestling arena.

A few days later, while sitting alone outside the tent and watching the setting sun, you were surprised yet joyful with the appearance of Emmanuel. He was covered in dust with a small bundle strapped across his shoulder. He told you of bad experiences in the hands of the authorities and how he managed to escape from them. He spoke with fear of the police as unbelievers once feared the rack.

The following days, Mamadou Njie, a UNHCR local employee wanted you to bribe him either by cash or in kind in order to get the official UNHCR refugee card. As you were contemplating on how to respond to him, you and Emmanuel received the UNHCR refugee card through the help of an American by the name of Sally White. She was one of the commission's resettlement programme employees who ultimately took charge of your case.

Once upon a time, in the middle of the night, a Range Rover SUV drove up to an isolated tent in the refugee camp. Masked men jumped out of the van and began spraying bullets. When they had done with shooting they set fire to the tent and drove off. From the ash, other refugees, who claimed it was an unprovoked violence, pulled the burned bodies of three men. In your delirium, you became more and more pessimistic of life in the refugee camp. Since your childhood, you repudiated violence with all your heart and soul. Once again you said to Emmanuel, "We must leave this place." In a wave of panic, as though death was at your heels, both of you gathered your belongings and left the refugee camp for Serekunda, where you hoped to get assistance from an acquaintance.

On your way by commercial bus you travelled with a group of noisy passengers. Five of them were males and five were females in their twenties and thirties, dressed in blue jeans and colourful Tee-shirts. They spoke the Wolof language and laughed loudly. Every little joke seemed to amuse them. They spoke of themselves being Serekunda natives and rock-solid Gambians. They became vulgar and boisterous, having no regard for others in the bus. They gossiped about their friends. They talked about the European and American tourists in the beach resorts, about a particular bar that was once a funeral home. In their foolish display of public nuisance, it seemed as if each of them wanted attention from the other. Neither the bus driver nor anybody else in the vehicle could ask them to be quiet for fear of arousing their anger. Your silence only opened the way to oblivion. Until the journey ended, there was no way you and Emmanuel could have avoided those nincompoops.

✠ ✠ ✠

A couple of months later, you rented a room in Serekunda. At times you visited Kololi which was a resort town on the shore of the Atlantic Ocean. It was surrounded by the Bijilo Forest. The primary hotels were located on "The Strip", a short road leading to the beach and the hotels of Senegambia and the Kairaba. Reminding yourself that wasting one's time was a sin, you engaged in the tie-dye fabric business while Emmanuel became a secondary school teacher of African History. Being gainfully employed and keeping a healthy mind became some of your priorities. As you waited for the Australian resettlement programme to materialize, your thoughts could not stop drifting into the nebulous future. At times you could not control your temper tantrums, especially when you were dejected or harassed by officials. So, you spent most of your social life attending theater performances by the Freetong Players group and watching Nigerian movies.

In the days that followed, doubt and fear of the immigration authorities led you to acquire the resident permit. Unlike most refugees, who could not afford it, for 1500 dalasi (about US$53) you could get yourself and Emmanuel the permit. You would not want to endure that humiliating house to house search by the Gambian police for refugees without identification cards. Just the other day, an acquaintance of Emmanuel was arrested, imprisoned, and forced to pay 125 dalasi (US$5) fine for not having proper identification. After the incident, he lamented that his five years stay in The Gambia was fruitless and worrisome. His dreams of receiving asylum in Europe or North America and his earlier reluctance, like others, to return home during a cease-fire were now history. Several months later, he told Emmanuel and yourself how he had enrolled in the UNHCR voluntary repatriation program to Sierra Leone before it ceased operation.

He pointed out that the UNHCR was going to stop giving out all forms of assistance to Sierra Leonean and Liberian refugees. These include food, medical treatment, and education. On the other hand, the organization's repatriation programme will offer an air ticket with 40 kilogram of baggage, free transportation to the host town in Sierra Leone, rice and cooking oil rations for six months. You wished him well, and expressed your continuing hope of being resettled with your sister in Australia. And so with time, you witnessed how forcible repatriation became one of the cardinal sins in dealing with refugees. For many new comers, the only offence was that they came too late.

✖ ✖ ✖

One day, during a student demonstration in the capital city Banjul and the town of Serekunda, angry students went on the rampage, burning government vehicles and buildings. Police were believed to have fired live ammunition on the demonstrators. Some students were shot dead by the police for perpetrating violence in the guise of demonstrating against the high cost of living. The next day, there was an uneasy calm as policemen in pick-up vehicles patrolled the streets to maintain order. Many worried and grieving refugee parents and relatives gathered around the city's mortuary for news about their missing or dead children. A large number of arrests were made and the government announced the indefinite closure of all schools and colleges. Several high school students were also arrested. They were alleged to have burnt down an office of the ruling political party. Parents were asked to keep their students at home until further notice, and the Gambia's security forces were put on maximum alert. You believed that such unfortunate events would be rare if only governments officials could stop being corrupt and provide their people with the basic social amenities.

This event reminded you of similar student unrest in Freetown, and more so of one of your former bosses at the bank who was in prison for corruption at a time when the nation was at war. Before he lost respect for stealing the bank blind, he was the chairman of the Board of Directors. It was rumoured that he was a thief even during his school days. Others said that he cheated in every high school and university examinations. At the bank, he became the toast of all ladies. He was never caught.

Corruption was pandemic in the country, so putting his hand in the bank till was not at all a big deal. But the rate at which he was doing this and with so much freedom was what infuriated others. So one day he was caught and sentenced to a mere twenty-four months in jail, while other common thieves who stole just a fraction of what he squandered were sentenced to fifty or more years in jail. A frown creased your face at the thought of such injustice. You would not want to return to that bank nor the country anymore. Your hope of resettlement with your sister in Australia was your only salvation.

When you received the news from UNHCR that your resettlement application had been approved, you were at the Serekunda market selling tie-and-dye fabric. At first, you could not believe the voice over the telephone. Either because it sounded calm or the news came suddenly. It was only after the person introduced herself as Sally White, your resettlement case officer, did you feel joy in achieving your goal.

The resettlement package was complete with air ticket and money as allowance to see you through the first two weeks. When you informed your twin sister, Joyce, in Brisbane, Australia, she screamed "Hallelujah." However, your joy was marred with sadness as you realized that you were going to be separated from Emmanuel. Meanwhile, your next goal was to sponsor him to join you in the Land Down Under.

12

Eternal Bliss

"We're under rebel attack," stammered Payma Kawa on hearing the sound of sporadic gunshots.

"I don't believe it. It's probably the gunshots of the peace-keeping soldiers," replied Niawa Lenga, Payma's wife who had just turned eighteen.

As the gunfire intensified, screams of children and women could be heard.

"I say we're under rebel attack," Payma repeated, raising himself from their conjugal mud bed with lightning speed for a tall man with a big frame.

"You're such a coward," said Niawa. "What kind of militia are you?"

The gunshots and screams sounded closer and Payma started to put on some clothes. A primary school drop-out in his mid-twenties, he had become a prosperous farmer, and had joined the government-backed militia opposed to the rebellion.

"Haven't you heard people talking of an impending attack by rebels?" said Payma, impatiently.

"But the peace-keeping force is just down the road," she said with weak conviction. Niawa's relaxed at-home air, her petite cocoa-dark complexion figure and long cornrow braids had always been admired by Payma who was jet-black in complexion.

In order to satisfy his curiosity, Payma peeped through the wooden window for a glimpse outdoors. To his surprise, from afar, he saw in an uneven line numerous flashes of what might have been flash lights being carried by people descending the hill that lay adjacent to the village. He asked Niawa to get ready to flee as he was pretty sure that they were being attacked by rebels.

"Oh, we're doomed," she dabbed tears from her eyes with her head-tie and wondered when she would ever get peace and joy to enjoy life. Joy was what she wanted most in her marriage. She let out a series of sobs that scared Payma into thinking she might go into a seizure. His message had gone straight into her heart. In haste, they started packing some of their few personal belongings into bundles.

Niawa and Payma had slept together for the first time as a newly-married couple in an atmosphere of love, cherished by the cool night wind. Payma's mud house with thatched roof in the village of Valunia had never been so cozy. Even though there was no moonlight, the previous night had been one of celebration. They had spent the whole day performing their marriage ceremony and visiting relatives and friends. The marriage also coincided with festivities of the beginning of the farming season. The occasion was marked by prayers, feasting and dancing. The couple went to bed exhausted until the blanket of night slowly uncovered itself to a new day.

Although husband and wife, like most other villagers, were skeptical about the worsening crisis in the country, yet they hoped that this year's harvest would be better than the previous ones. They have heard of merchants of war, dressed in uniforms of brutality, obsessed with the idea of creating a better country while riding roughshod over human rights. They had heard how these soldiers of fortune stifled the freedoms of the weak and dispossessed they claimed to be attempting to redeem from post-colonial bondage.

Niawa was still dabbing tears from her eyes as the couple ran out of their houses to join other fleeing villagers, some of whose houses were already in flames. Few had the time to leave with any personal belongings. Family members became separated from each other. Niawa wondered what would have become of her parents living on the other side of the village. The rebels opened fire at everything; people, animals, and inanimate objects. It was massacre time. While some rebels shouted *One Love* and gave each other exuberant high fives, others shouted *Operation No Living Thing*. Most of them were nothing more than gun fodder for war lords; young boys and girls being fed myths disguised as truths.

Niawa, Payma, and some other villagers were abducted by the rebels. Like other abductees, their feet and hands were bound with wire and they were matched to the village square, where they were forced to sit on the ground. Most of the rebels were half-naked, with belts of bullets criss-crossing their torsos. Others wore wigs on their heads and dark sunglasses.

Niawa was dragged into the nearby bush. She screamed and struggled to free herself from the iron-grips of three sneering, grim-faced rebels. With her back on the ground, they wasted no time. She was unable to break free from them until they have satisfied their erotic desires. For a brief moment, fear glistened in her watery eyes as she waited to see the three men retreat. She was left in tears and pain. She blinked away her tears and staggered deep into the bush heading towards the motor road.

✄ ✄ ✄

Back in the village square, the rebels were brutalizing the other abductees.

"Are there any militia among you?" questioned one of the rebels who looked like their leader. As nobody replied, he shouted his question and kicked Payma viciously on his left side. Payma grunted like a pig being led to the slaughter house.

"You're all going to be killed except the militias who would join us in our struggle to win this war." He clenched his teeth with determination, "I mean those of you who would glorify and mythologize our manifesto."

Without hesitation Payma responded in a trembling voice, "I'm a militia." His heart pounded against his chest like a pestle in a mortar.

"Good man," said the rebel, untying his feet and asking Payma to step aside.

As far as Payma was concerned, the war was one in which tribalism was being used to validate politics. He believed that it was a war that would have neither victor nor vanquish. It was a war that reflected the futility of the endeavours of its mongers. Although he had seen scores of displaced people passing through his village with rumours of war, Payma had long since made up his mind not to leave.

Since then, he had felt inordinately proud to be a member of the government-backed militia; a revered, though in some quarters, infamous group. He never thought of disassociating himself from the so-called values of the group who were known to harass and ostracize those they considered to be nincompoops and rebel sympathizers.

Like his comrades, Payma would join the government troops to perform murder and mayhem; going beyond simple acceptance and knowingly drawing the wrath of the rebels. Payma remembered conniving with his comrades to murder a teenage girl they suspected of being a rebel. That event never bothered him, and he still felt superior for having been given the task of using a machete to slash the arteries at the back of the girls' ankles.

With the village under siege, his only hope was to abjure his allegiance to the militia and join the rebels.

"Are there any more militias ready to join us?" the rebel leader asked as he mopped sweat away from his forehead.

A few more male and female abductees responded positively. As their feet were untied, they too were asked to join Payma's group. Then the rebel leader shouted a command, *Operation!* Within a twinkle of an eye, a volley of bullets was fired into the group killing Payma and the others.

✕ ✕ ✕

On the other side of the village, Niawa continued to stagger through the bush towards the motor road. Thoughts of her childhood days passed through her mind in rapid succession. She was born in the village of Fo Mile near Waterloo, which was about twenty-four miles from Freetown. She grew up as a child in this village with her mother, Janet. Later, as a young girl, she was raised by her elder sister Fabianne in the town of Bauya, which once boasted of a major provincial railway station.

Niawa detested the idea of serving as a nanny to Fabianne's baby boy instead of going to school. Like most African girls of her age, her daily chores included fetching water, firewood, washing the dishes, sweeping, and food preparation. Formal primary schooling for her was pursued infrequently in over-crowded classes where corporal punishment was not uncommon, and studying at night with the help of a kerosene lamp or candle was usual.

It was only when she joined her parents in Freetown that she was able to continue regular schooling that led her up to the first form at the Methodist Girls High School. She became a member of the school choir. She was told that her voice was a mix of Mariam Makeba and *La Femme Chic-Choc* Oumou Dioubate. She fervently practiced athletics during her school days, winning many racing contests, and excelling to glorious heights in her class. Naiwa's schooling was cut short after just one year in secondary school because her parents could not afford to pay her school fees. Hence, it was merely by chance that she got married to Payma.

As she headed towards the motor road, she was rudely awakened from her thoughts when she heard the sound of a motor vehicle. She must have walked in the bush for a very long distance as it was already dusk. Niawa doubled her foot steps in order to reach the road and catch up with the vehicle. She arrived just in time to flag its driver.

Moments later, she found herself squeezed in the truck with other passengers like sardines in a tin. The smell of human sweat combined with the stench of raw and dried fish filled the air. Overflowing bags of cassava and potatoes lost some of their contents as the truck galloped in the numerous potholes, and hurtled along the lonely road towards Freetown. It was the month of March, the peak period of the dry season, and so the road was dusty. The cool breeze in her face and the fatigue in her body coaxed her to sleep instantly.

Then she dreamt that a hefty-looking mermaid and a dreaded masquerade from the female secret society were chasing her through a bush path. They wanted to initiate her into the society. She ran, and ran, and ran, until she arrived at a brook where some young girls were bathing while others were doing their laundry. The girls stopped what they were doing and started laughing at her being chased by a mermaid and a masquerade.

She woke up from her dream to the sound of a volley of AK-47 gunshots ringing through the air and forcing the truck to come to an abrupt stop. Niawa and some other passengers screamed in fear.

"Everybody out!" shouted a young woman in civilian attire and a military fatigue cap, gesturing at the passengers with her rifle. They started disembarking from the truck.

"This is a rebel hold-up," she continued, and thereafter gave the truck driver a solid kick on his buttocks that sent him reeling into the group of rebels. The rebels burst into laughter and started kicking, punching and requesting money from him.

Niawa became confused as her heart missed a beat. She felt warm urine dripping down her thighs. She shivered in fear at the thought of being abducted by rebels. The urge to bolt for her life passed her mind. But she had heard stories of how deadly it could be for a fool attempting to flee from rebels. If only they could just take what they wanted and leave them alone, she thought.

The rebels marched all the passengers into the nearby forest which echoed the chirping sounds of crickets. Startled by the procession of abductees, the owls went haywire with their hair-raising hoots. As though scampering for safety, the moon disappeared, leaving the forest as dark as a grave. Surely this was truly a harbinger of evil things to come, Niawa thought.

They were tied in groups of four and forced to march for hours through the night. Divided into smaller groups, they were then taken to different locations. Their captors threatened them with death if they tried to flee or disobey. Niawa watched as some abductees were beaten to death with clubs and butts of guns. Those who were unable to keep up with the hours of marching were hacked to death with machetes. There was little or no food and water. Raw rice and cassava were rationed among them. After a week in captivity, Niawa learnt from her fellow abductees that although they were abducted at a checkpoint called Lumpa, they were now miles away in an area called Devil Hole.

✕ ✕ ✕

Early one morning during the second week of their abduction, the rebels gathered all their female abductees in the deserted village square and asked them to disrobe. Once the women were all nude, some of the high-ranking rebels took off their jackets and threw them into a heap in front of the women. One by one, they asked each woman to randomly pick a jacket from the heap and raise it up like a banner. The rebel to whom the jacket belonged would then take the woman as his wife. Niawa ended up with a dirty-looking man by the name of Captain Blood, an ugly and ruthless young man who hardly spoke. He immediately escorted her into an abandoned hut and raped her several times for the rest of the day. She could not resist his insatiable sexual demands for fear of being beaten or killed.

Captain Blood, otherwise called Lahai Jusu, was born in a prison by a female inmate who was serving a life sentence for murdering her spouse. He was raised by foster parents who later rejected him because he was troublesome, played truancy during primary schooling, and spent most of his time gambling and smoking in his adolescence.

Though a taciturn fellow, he was a great orator when it came to communicating the rebellion's propaganda. Few hours after committing his gruesome act on Niawa, Captain Blood stood before the abductees, absolutely confident to give a speech. He spoke in Krio:

"For the past five years you idiots have referred to us as mere marauding rebels-cum-freedom fighters. As far as we're concerned, the war was brought about largely by the lack of social amenities and the rampant practice of greed and corruption. Since the country gained political independence fifty years ago, you appeared to be very much self-centred, highly-possessive, and complacent. Little or no achievements were recorded within this lengthy and depressive period."

At this Captain Blood's comrades shouted in unison: "Yeah!"

He continued his speech with increasing vigour:

"While some of you thought that you were superior to others, some sought to perpetrate societal degradation. Successive governments, whether colonial, democratic, or military could not provide food, basic primary health care, clean water supply, electricity and education for us. So we'll continue to fight until we win. We're disgruntled and tired of this system." Captain Blood ended his speech to applause from his comrades.

Under the tutelage of Captain Blood, the rebels taught their abductees the basics of guerilla warfare. Firstly, they flogged them methodically with canes, and then taught them how to use weapons. As the days went by Niawa became weak and disoriented due to the abuse meted out to her already stressed mind. She could hardly carry a gun, let alone learn how to shoot. She was routinely drugged, raped, and forced by Captain Blood to prepare his food and do his laundry. He yearned to see her beg for mercy, a sign that unerringly showed his victim's breakdown and desire for redemption. Indeed, Niawa had breakdowns and begged for mercy on a daily basis, but they were met with only the ridicules of triumphant contempt from him. She prayed for death hoping that it would bring her joy.

The camp was always on the move for fear of being detected by the government forces and militias. Whenever time permitted, the rebels would relax, drink, eat, smoke, and laugh boisterously. They listened to news on transistor radios and talked about the situations being reported. They would enumerate the atrocities of the government forces on rebel sympathizers among the civilian population. They spoke of how government soldiers and militias would displace people from towns and villages that were once under rebel control to far-away camps under the pretence of separating the people from the rebels. They showed their disgust and bitterness when they heard news blaming them for the war when in actual fact crimes were also committed by government soldiers and militias, whom the rebels termed wolves in sheep clothing.

And then one day, Niawa was awakened with a start by the bleating of a goat stolen by the rebels. One could tell by Niawa's squint that her mind was literally racing. Whenever she was juggling thoughts, she narrowed her eyes. The more cluttered her mind, the narrower her eyes became. It was almost dawn but the sun was yet to rise. She was getting ready to fetch water from a nearby stream for Captain Blood.

All of a sudden, she heard the drone of a helicopter and shouts from the rebels commanding everyone to take cover. Then all hell was let loose as the helicopter gunship opened fire on them. The rebels responded by firing a rocket propelled grenade at the helicopter gunship but they missed their target. Grenades and rapid gunfire came from the helicopter. The area became smoky and dusty. The groans of the dying and the screams of the living could be heard. Everyone was running helter-skelter, trying to save their lives.

In the ensuing mayhem, Niawa's right leg was pierced by the protruding spike of a tree branch. From her dress, she tore a piece of cloth which she used to tie the wound, keeping it from bleeding. She hopped towards the stream, hardly able to bear the sensation of pain mingling with the anxiety that she would not escape from this mayhem unhurt. The slippers on her right foot flapped like a jawbone when she hopped.

Heading downstream, she followed its bank, taking cover in bushes and behind trees. Although she was thirsty, exhausted and drenched in sweat she did not dare to stop as she could still hear the sound of gunshots and grenades. She startled a troop of monkeys that were playing by the stream. They jumped and ran into the bush chattering noisily, and making Niawa quake with fear. At the same time, she wished that she could just stop running and bathe in the stream. However, she kept hopping for about one hour until she arrived in a deserted village with just seven huts.

By now she was weary and footsore. She wondered if she could take a break in one of the huts but then a sick feeling gripped her at the thoughts of the humiliation of rape, hunger, fear, and death. No, she must keep going, she told herself. She kept hopping faster under the warm tropical morning sun.

Scared out of her wits, she stared ahead without seeing anything. It was due to one of those designs of fate that Niawa managed to arrive in a town where she saw war-displaced people pushing and shoving each other to climb on the back of an open truck that had seen better days. She joined in the struggle when she learnt that it was a government-owned truck offering a free ride to Freetown. A few hours later, she was on board the truck speeding dangerously and trying to avoid the pot-holes that covered its dusty track. Niawa could not believe that she had escaped from the rebels.

⚔ ⚔ ⚔

In the following days, she found herself in a refugee camp from where she was taken to a hospital. The doctor told her that her right leg had become infected with gangrene and as such it must be amputated in order to save her life. Niawa felt devastated and cried endlessly. She wondered why life seemed to be making a mockery of her. All along, she thought she wanted just peace and joy to enjoy life but since her marriage to Payma, her life has been fraught with misfortune. Once her leg was amputated, she had a hunch that life was not worth living. She prayed for death and eternal bliss.

⚅ ⚅ ⚅

One morning before sunrise, Niawa was hopping along the bush path from a nearby stream that led to the refugee camp. Then, momentarily, she felt like she was going to die. Her view became blurred, and her skinny body shivered. In her reverie, she saw an old woman with both legs missing. The crutch underneath Niawa's right armpit squeaked at every footstep like an unoiled hinge. The pot of water on her head became unbearable to carry.

At first cockcrow, Niawa arrived at the camp shivering and went to bed immediately. She tried to calm down but the spasms from repeated vomiting and excessive perspiration became painful. She gasped for breath but in vain. She felt the presence of the angel of death standing over her helpless body like the sword of Damocles, asking:

"Who are you?"

She muttered, "I'm a God-fearing person."

Thereafter, without any further ado, the angel gently took away Niawa's life. Like a dream, Niawa's soul heard her acquaintances wailing over her corpse, and talking about holding a wake. She wished they could just convey her to the cemetery without weeping or a wake.

There was a funeral procession accompanied by the appropriate dirge but with neither a eulogy nor an epitaph at the cemetary. Niawa was buried the same day before sunset. In her grave, she heard the footfalls of the mourners leaving the graveyard. Then, an electrifying flash of lightning shed light on her and the angel of death reappeared:

"Resurrect and go wherever you want as the Day of Judgment is yet to come!" the angel commanded.

Like a bird soaring in the easterlies, Niawa's soul went home to her family. She saw and heard the living and the dead but the living could not see or hear her. She came across hundreds of other souls heading breezily in different directions. In a state of total incommunicado, they hastily repelled each other like opposite poles of a magnet. They all appeared in white flowing shrouds, neither male nor female, devoid of any form of eye contact. Some appeared as pallbearers, others were carrying urns. A few were standing by a pyre getting ready to disinter a body.

Niawa's soul arrived at a relative's home to find another soul, a beautiful woman, mourning among the living. She was also in white flowing shroud. The woman beckoned to her as if to say, "Come to me." But Niawa could not understand the woman. By gesturing three times, the woman pointed to Niawa and then to the sun.

Niawa's soul began to move towards the sun. The laughter of death bellowed in her ears. As she got closer to the sun, it became a valley of resurrected souls. While some were taking the right-hand path, others went left. She took the left-hand path and found herself among greedy-guts fighting to eat the flesh of one another, and throwing their bones into a raging inferno. Three of these gluttons appeared as gravediggers pushing a sarcophagus onto a grave. When they saw Niawa, they stopped what they were doing and grabbed her by her hair. They hurled her into the inferno, uninterested in devouring her.

With only a head and two hands, no torso, she found herself falling into an abyss. Her hands became mouths; one single eye stood on her forehead wide-open like the head-lamp of a hunter. While her left mouth narrated all her wrong-doings, her right mouth sang songs of praise. She kept falling deeper and deeper until her soul changed into a white dove and soared out of the abyss onto a mountain.

From her bird's eye-view, while perching on a rock, Niawa saw a deep valley below her in the form of a beautiful garden with flowers blossoming and different fruits dangling from golden branches. She saw a river of milk and honey flowing towards a magnificent waterfall. The hot sun shone brightly creating a rainbow around the falls. Niawa heard the chirping of birds, the roaring of lions, the trumpeting of elephants, and felt the gentle breeze of eternal bliss.

✄ ✄ ✄

To order more copies of this book, find books by other
Canadian authors, or make inquiries about publishing your own
book, contact PageMaster at:

PageMaster Publication Services Inc.
11340-120 Street, Edmonton, AB T5G 0W5
books@pagemaster.ca
780-425-9303

catalogue and e-commerce store
www.ShopPageMaster.ca

About the Author

Bakar Mansaray, MBA, is a Canadian author of Sierra Leonean descent. His work includes essays and short stories. Essays: *Multiculturalism, an Afro-Canadian Heritage* (Diversity Magazine, 2015); *My Dream for the Future of Christian Fiction in Sierra Leone* (Christian Monthly Library - West Africa, 2013); *The Past, Current and Future State of African and Caribbean Writing and Publishing* (Ayebia, 2011); *Education in Sierra Leone: An Analysis* (The Patriotic Vanguard, 2009). *Short Stories: Eternal Bliss* (Ndi-Diaspora - ICAE, 2014); *Mud House Thatched Roof; 7:20 in the Morning; The Escape* (The Patriotic Vanguard, 2008). Bakar is a member of the Writers' Guild of Alberta, Canada. He is at work on a novel as part of his entertaining Mandingo Scrolls Series.

His blog can be viewed at www.mandingoscrolls.blogspot.com
Follow Bakar on:
Facebook (Mandingo Scrolls)
Twitter (Mandingo Scrolls)